A LIFE-CH

Several years ago I received
remember who wrote it, only w

Dear Dr. Wheeler,

I have a big favor to ask y... all, though, I want you to know how much I enjoy your story collections; they have greatly enriched my life. Now for the favor: I was wondering if you have any interest in doing with books what you are doing with stories.

You see, while I love to read, I haven't the slightest idea of where to start. There are millions of books out there, and most of them—authors too—are just one big blur to me. I want to use my time wisely, to choose books which will not only take me somewhere but also make me a better and kinder person.

I envy you because you know which books are worth reading and which are not. Do you possibly have a list of worthy books that you wouldn't mind sending to me?

I responded to this letter, but most inadequately, for at that time I had no such list. I tried to put the plea behind me, but it dug in its heels and kept me awake at night. Eventually, I concluded that a Higher Power was at work here and that I needed to do something about it. I put together a proposal for a broad reading plan based on books I knew and loved—books that had powerfully affected me, that had opened other worlds and cultures to me, and that had made me a kinder, more empathetic person.

But that letter writer had asked for more than just a list of titles. She wanted me to introduce her to the authors of these books, to their lives and their times. To that end, I've included in the introduction to each story in this series a biographical sketch of the author to help the reader appreciate the historical, geographical, and cultural contexts in which a story was written. Also, as a long-time teacher, I've always found study-guide questions to be indispensable in helping readers to understand more fully the material they're reading, hence my decision to incorporate discussion questions for each chapter in an afterword at the end of the book. Finally, since I love turn-of-the-century woodcut illustrations, I've tried to incorporate as many of these into the text as possible.

There is another reason for this series—perhaps the most important. Our hope is that it will encourage thousands of people to fall in love with reading, as well as help them to discover that a life devoid of emotional, spiritual, and intellectual growth is not worth living.

Welcome to our expanding family of wordsmiths, of people of all ages who wish to grow daily, to develop to the fullest the talents God lends to each of us—people who believe as does Robert Browning's persona in *Andrea del Sarto:*

Ah, but a man's reach should exceed his grasp,
Or what's a heaven for?

Joe Wheeler

Note: The books in this series have been selected because they are among the finest literary works in history. However, you should be aware that some content might not be suitable for all ages, so we recommend you review the material before sharing it with your family.

YOU HANG IT ON THE TREE, ANGELINA

FOCUS ON THE FAMILY®
Great Stories

The Christmas Angel

by
Abbie Farwell Brown

Introduction and Afterword by
Joe Wheeler, Ph.D.

Tyndale House Publishers, Wheaton, Illinois

THE CHRISTMAS ANGEL

Library of Congress Cataloging-in-Publication Data
Brown, Abbie Farwell, d. 1927.
The Christmas angel / by Abbie Farwell Brown ; introduction and afterword by Joe Wheeler.
p. cm. — (Focus on the Family great stories)
Includes bibliographical references.
ISBN 1-56179-762-6
I. Wheeler, Joe L., 1936 II. Title. III. Series.
PS3503.R78 C48 1999
813'.52—dc21 99-32202
CIP

A Focus on the Family book published by Tyndale House Publishers, Wheaton, Illinois.

The illustrations in this book are by Reginald B. Birch, from the Houghton Mifflin Company 1910 edition of *The Christmas Angel.* All illustrations are from the library of Joe Wheeler.

Joe Wheeler is represented by the literary agency of Alive Communications, 1465 Kelly Johnson Blvd., Suite 320, Colorado Springs, CO 80920.

Cover design by Candi Park D'Agnese
Cover photo of angel by Tim O'Hara Photography, Inc.
Cover photo of house by Peter Gridley, FPG International
Cover photo of toys and letters by ©1999 PhotoDisc, Inc.

Printed in the United States of America

99 00 01 02 03 04 05 06/10 9 8 7 6 5 4 3 2 1

Table of Contents

List of Illustrations

Introduction

ABBIE FARWELL BROWN AND *THE CHRISTMAS ANGEL*

I have always loved Christmas stories—especially the heart-tugging kind. And let's face it, sentiment and Christmas belong together. Of all the seasons of the year, the heart is the most open to love, empathy, kindness, forgiveness, generosity, and change . . . at Christmas.

Thousands of authors have written stories about Christmas, but sadly, most of them are shallow, sterile, and unmoving. These stories may be technically brilliant, but if they fail to engage the heart, I view them as failures.

Only a few have written "great" Christmas stories, and even fewer have written "great" Christmas books (usually novelette length rather than full book length, as Christmas books are rarely very long). And of those few *special* Christmas books which percolate to the top, very few manage to stay there, but gradually, over time, sink down into that vast subterranean sea of forgotten books. To stay alive, season after season, generation after generation, presupposes a magical ingredient no critic-scientist has ever been able to isolate. *The Christmas Carol, Miracle on 34th Street, It's a Wonderful Life,* and *The Other Wise Man* have made it. In recent years, *The Best Christmas Pageant Ever* by Barbara Robinson (1972) and Richard Paul Evans' *The Christmas Box* (1993) have so far evidenced staying power, but only time will reveal whether they will stay there.

But, none of this precludes comebacks. Literature and public taste are, after all, cyclical, thus even during authors' lifetimes, reputations roll along on roller-coasters, undulating up and down as public tastes and demands change. No one remains *hot* forever. But sometimes certain works brazenly dig into our memories and impudently refuse to leave. Which brings us to Abbie Farwell Brown.

It was some years ago when I first "met" her. My wife and I were wandering around New England at the height of fall colors. While browsing in a used bookstore, Connie discovered an old book—and short—with the intriguing title of *The Christmas Angel.* She brought it over to me and asked if I was familiar with it or with the author. I was not, but on the strength of the wonderful woodcut illustrations, we bought it. Upon our return home, I unpacked it, then sat down to read it—and *LOVED* it.

So here it is. I don't often creep out far enough on limbs to risk getting sawed off, but I shall make an exception for *The Christmas Angel.* It has all the enduring qualities that has kept *The Christmas Carol* at the top for over a century and a half—in fact, one manuscript reader told me that she even *prefers* it over *The Christmas Carol.* It is one of those rarities: a book that should be loved equally by *all* generations—from small children to senior citizens. I can see it being filmed; and I can see it becoming a Christmas tradition: unthinkable to get through a Christmas season without reading it out loud to the family once again.

Since the story is divided into 15 short chapters, it would lend itself to being spread out during Advent or the twelve days of Christmas. Having said that, I'll prophesy that pressure to read on by the listeners might make a proposed timetable difficult to stick with.

And, unquestionably, the Reginald Birch illustrations add a very special dimension to the book.

When Christ wished to hammer home a point, He told a story, a parable, an allegory. This is just such a story. But, coupled with that is something else: It is one of the most memorable and poignant angel stories I have ever read. And it is amazing how many people today are rediscovering angel stories!

In this story, the angel's "target" is Miss Terry—a bitter, cold, bigoted, and unforgiving old woman. As with Dickens's Scrooge, in her life virtually all sentiment, caring, and love had been discarded, then trampled on, in her morose journey through the years. And now, at Christmas, but one tie to her past remains, one key that might unlock her cell of isolation: her childhood box of toys.

She determines to burn them—*every last one.*

About the Introduction

For decades, one of the few absolutes in my literature classes has been this: *Never read the introduction before reading the book!* Those who ignored my thundering admonition lived to regret their disobedience. Downcast, they would come to me and say, "Dr. Wheeler, I confess that I read the introduction first, and it wrecked the book for me. I couldn't enjoy the story, because all the way through, I saw it through someone *else's* eyes. I don't agree with the editor on certain points, but those conclusions are in my head, and now I don't know *what* I think!"

Given that God never created a human clone, no two of us will ever perceive reality in exactly the same way—and no two of us ever should! Therefore, no matter how educated, polished, brilliant, insightful, or eloquent the teacher might be, don't ever permit that person to tell you how to think or respond, for that is a violation of the most sacred thing God gives us—our individuality.

My solution to the introduction problem was to split it in two: an introduction, to whet the appetite for, and enrich the reading of, the book; and an afterword, to generate discussion and debate *after* the reader has arrived at his or her own conclusions about the book and is ready to challenge my (the teacher's) perceptions.

About the Illustrations

For well over half a century, *St. Nicholas Magazine* was the premier children's magazine in America, and its editor, Mary Mapes Dodge, a household name. Almost as famous during the last quarter of the nineteenth century and first quarter of the twentieth was artist Reginald Birch, whose illustrations appeared in virtually every issue of *St. Nicholas Magazine*, and in many children's books as well. His romanticized Little Lord Fauntleroy look—Birch did the illustrations for the original book—dominated contemporary children's art just as much as Norman Rockwell would after him.

Readers of this series will already be familiar with Birch because of the memorable half-tone illustrations he did for Louisa May Alcott's *Little Men*. These however are woodcuts, among the finest Birch ever did, completely capturing the mood and characters in this remarkable story.

About the Author
Abbie Farwell Brown (1871–1927)

No matter what my birth may be,
No matter where my lot is cast
I am the heir in equity
Of all the wondrous past.

The art, the science, and the lore
Of all the ages long since dust,
The wisdom of the world in store
Is mine, all mine, in trust.

The beauty of the living earth,
The power of the golden sun,
The present, whatsoever my birth,
I share with everyone.

As much as any man, am I
The owner of the working day,
Mine are the minutes as they fly
To save or throw away.

And mine the future to be greater
Unto the generation new
I help to shape it with my breath
Mine as I think or do.

Present and past my heritage
The future laid in my control,
No matter what my name or age
I am a master-soul.

—Abbie Farwell Brown, "The Heritage," 1919,
archived in the Schlesinger Library at Radcliffe

Without question, this biography has proved to be the hardest one yet to research and write. In fact, for a time, I had all but resigned myself to there being no life sketch of her at all! But we persisted, and finally struck pay dirt: The Schlesinger Library of Radcliffe College at Harvard University houses all that apparently exists of Abbie Farwell Brown's papers.

Thus to Cambridge, Massachusetts I journeyed, and found my way to the white-porticoed Schlesinger Library at Radcliffe, Brown's alma mater. They take very good care of the three small boxes of her papers.

Barbara Haber (head curator of books and manuscripts) and Wendy Thomas were especially helpful and kind to me, not only helping me with manuscripts and archival materials but also launching me out upon the Internet. Extremely helpful in conceptualizing Miss Brown's story is the life synopsis, written by Jo Ann Abraham Reiss, and Carolyn Ticknor's splendid eulogy, "Carolyn Ticknor's Estimate of Abbie Farwell Brown," March 23, 1927, Boston newspaper column (both archived in the Schlesinger Library of Radcliffe). If this modest biography is effective, Barbara Haber and her equally helpful associates made what you are now reading possible. So, bless them!

There is no biography to work from. Even though Brown was a faithful diarist, only two diaries survive—and they are more travelogue than diary. Neither did her letters survive her, of which she wrote thousands. I might have known this would be so, for in a column she wrote (under a pseudonym) in 1898, when she was only 27, are these prophetic words: "I shall have a big bonfire tonight on my open hearth. I have been looking over piles and heaps of old letters this morning, sorting them out and trying to decide which were really worth keeping and which had served their brief purpose and were better metamorphosed into ashes."

As a result of no diaries, and no letters to speak of, I am forced to write a very different kind of life sketch. I will have to let her own words do the speaking; thoughts will prevail over actions.

A New England Princess

The blood royal of America is *Mayflower*ian. Many other ships brought settlers, in the earliest days, to places such as St. Augustine, Roanoke, Jamestown, Baltimore, Philadelphia, and New Amsterdam, but only the *Mayflower* registers in the American consciousness as the first, as the true beginning of things.

The little girl who cried her way into Boston's Brahminic Beacon Hill, thirteen generations later, carried in her tiny veins the bluest blood in New England. Her father, Benjamin Farwell Brown, was descended from

Isaac Allerton, a *Mayflower* settler, who had served as assistant governor of the Plymouth Colony. Her mother, Clara Neal Brown, came from a family of New Hampshire pioneers who had settled and named the town of Exeter. For ten generations, not one of little Abbie's ancestors had lived outside New England. Her lineage included Cavaliers, Roundheads, Puritans, Church of Englanders, explorers, adventurers, sailors, farmers, leaders (including Captain Myles Standish), merchants, and writers, and reached all the way back to William the Conqueror. Abbie herself, with good reason, was called a "bluestocking."

She was born on August 21 of 1871 in the family home at 41 West Cedar Street. Everyone cooperated: The doctor arrived at half past three, the nurse around four, and Abbie—weighing eight pounds—before five. The robust appetite she was born with would quickly grow into an appetite for all life, all experience, all nature.

My Little Chair

I had a little arm-chair once; 'twas very, very small,
So no one else, but only I, could sit in it at all,
And by the open fireplace I'd watch the sparks arise,
While in the glowing embers came strange pictures to my eyes,—
My chin upon my chubby hand, my elbow on my knee,
And sitting in the little chair just big enough for me.

I saw fair towers and battlements, with moat and drawbridge too,
And fairy knights and ladies from the world my fancy knew,
And in the coals great caverns yawned, whence fiery dragons came,
With breath of sparks and cinders black and eyes of hot red flame.
Oh, they were very wonderful, the sights I used to see
When sitting in that little chair just big enough for me.

But now the magic spell is gone, and sadly, all in vain,
I look into the fire to see those pictures bright again;
But with the little chair I fear I have outgrown them all,
For one can only see the fairy world when one is small.
And as the fire cracks and snaps I long once more to be
A child, and in the little chair just big enough for me.

—Abbie Farwell Brown, "My Little Chair",
archived in the Schlesinger Library at Radcliffe

Her mother, educated at Hampton Academy, artistic, and an award-winning author herself, shaped her childhood, and that of her one sibling, Ethel. Looking back on those early days, Abbie observed, "I cannot remember when I did not write. My mother was always very clever with her pen and pencil. When my sister and I were tiny girls our mother started a little home paper for us. We called it the *Catkin*, being fond, as we all were, of cats. We wrote jingles and scraps of prose." ("Young Women Who Uphold Our Literary Fame Belong to the Galaxy of Stars," *Sunday Boston Herald*, January 10, 1904). Sometimes their mother illustrated it, but more often Abbie and Ethel did. Amazingly, these copies of the *Catkin*, now close to a century and a quarter old, survived. What an experience it was, after having read about them, to open a folder in the Schlesinger Library and pull out these hand-written, hand-illustrated family magazines. The paper being of high rag content, the illustrations look as if they could have been sketched only a short time ago, rather than but thirteen to fifteen years after the Civil War.

Her mother, having connections with leading magazines of the day, encouraged the little girls to set their sights high at a very early age. Thus both girls became known by readers of the greatest children's magazine of the age, *St. Nicholas* (Abbie writing and Ethel illustrating), while they were still in their early teens.

Abbie's formal schooling began at Bowdoin School, where she graduated as valedictorian in 1886 at the age of fourteen. Already we can see in that valedictory, her concern for all life; indeed her perception of the interconnectedness of life:

> Everything in nature is made for a purpose. The smallest living creature has its mission. The tiniest grain of sand has its part in forming the vast sea beds which sustain the weight of the ocean. The frail insect living but an hour fulfills its mission, and the largest animal on earth can do no more.
>
> The flowers,—have they not all missions? Does not one gladden our hearts with its beauty, another yield sweet perfume to please us, and another save our lives as a medicine?
>
> Then may we not each have a purpose, a higher motive, something more than to be content merely to

> drag along from day to day getting enough to eat and drink?
>
> May we not, like the columbine which, dressed in bright colors and dancing gaily on its slender stem, brightens and lends life to the grey old rock against which it grows, may we not lighten the burdens of some other human being like ourselves, perhaps less fortunate than we, but still a fellow creature and needing comfort like us? (excerpted from Brown's 1886 Valedictory, Bowdoin School, archived in the Schlesinger Library of Radcliffe)

Abbie may not at this time have fully realized her calling in life, nevertheless this valedictory clearly telegraphs what her life and writing would be all about. Note that her illustrations, her metaphoric imagery, comes straight from nature. That would always be so even after she reached full artistic maturity. Already she was developing the rhythm and beat that would give her prose and poetry such power and poignancy. Rather ironic, isn't it, that this child of one of America's greatest cities should draw almost exclusively from the rural and from nature for her subject matter and imagery.

Almost no author is able to retain childhood perspective once childhood is past. Elizabeth Goudge is one of the only such writers I have ever known who has been able to retain the lens of childhood after growing up. Abbie Farwell Brown is another, as we shall see. But "My Little Chair" reveals to us that it wasn't easy, retaining that low-to-the-ground perspective. Her unique italicized *asides* enable her to carry on dual conversations with her readers.

Points of View

When beating drums and tramping feet
With crowds of people fill the streets,
Oh how they run and push and cry
To watch the soldiers passing by!
But though I stand on tiptoe tall,
The grown-ups make a solid wall.
Oh, it is very sad to be
So little that one cannot see!

The procession invisible.

I hear the bands of music play,
And see some banners move away.
The soldiers pass and soon are gone,
And I have seen not even one! *Selfish*
The people must forget, I know, *big*
That they were children long ago. *folk!*
How splendid it must feel to be
So big that one can always see!

But sometimes when the grown-ups come
To see my play house here at home,
And when I try to show the rest
The things I like the very best,— *Blind*
The truly things one has to "play,"— *big*
They only look around and say, *folk!*
"I can't see any castle there!"
Or "Where's the Princess?" "How?" and "Where?"

Oh, does it not seem very queer
When I can see them plainly here,
Big people who could view so well
The long procession, and could tell *Good*
What uniform the soldiers wore, *to*
Can't see things on the nursery floor? *be*
How dreadful it must feel to be *little!*
So big and old one cannot see!

—Abbie Farwell Brown, from *A Pocketful of Posies,* 1902

Is childhood an accumulation of weeks, months, and years? Or is it a state of mind? What we *do* know is that children perceive life differently than adults do. Brown's view was perhaps best articulated during a newspaper interview: "Children could write juvenile masterpieces if grown people wouldn't prod them with models. . . . The trouble with most of the literature that is being written for children is that the writers know too much and admit that they know it.

"Most authors don't look at a cow as a child looks at a cow—horns and tail and a meadowy smell—but they must invariably see a dairy.

"Many writers turn to writing child stuff as a last resort of the editorial incompetent; whereas to get down on one's knees and take a waist-high view of life is a kind of literary acrobatics possible only to the patient" (excerpted from undated newspaper clipping, "Child Classics Seen By Author," archived in the Schlesinger Library of Radcliffe).

Following graduation from Bowdoin, Abbie enrolled in Boston Girls' Latin School,[1] where she gave birth to, organized, and edited the school paper, *The Jabberwock*, thereby revealing her love for Lewis Carroll's "Alice" books. It was during these years that Josephine Preston Peabody, descendant of another prominent New England family, came into her life. Josephine would not only become one of the nation's best known Boston poets, but she would also become the closest and dearest friend Abbie would ever know, a true soul sister.

These were full years for Abbie, as she was ever in the center of whatever activities were going on: be they dances, Dickens carnivals, banquets, masques and plays, parades, prize drills, or calisthenics. Along the way she somehow found time to add to her growing national recognition as an author by her submissions to magazines such as *St. Nicholas*. *The Jabberwock* saw most of these literary labors first, however. In 1891, Abbie was elected president of her graduating class.

Then came Radcliffe, then and now one of the most prestigious women's colleges in America. She attended there during the years 1891–2 and 1893–4, taking, as always, a most active part in campus dramatics and literary affairs, and continuing to find homes for her poems and stories.

An Immune

From all accounts, the talented Miss Brown was lovely, and always the center of a flock of devoted admirers, men *and* women. Clearly, she had many opportunities to marry, but took advantage of none of them—in fact, she would live her entire life in the house on West Cedar Street in which she was born.

Since she left no revealing diary entries or letters, in terms of her

---

1 Latin schools were liberal arts oriented but with a classical literature—especially Latin—base. Students in those days rarely learned any other contemporary language besides English.

romantic relationships, we are forced to look for clues in her writings, always a dangerous thing to do, for one's fictional world does not necessarily mirror the author's actual life. One poem especially, written during her first year at Radcliffe, quite likely was autobiographical.

Sic Transit

I had a castle in the air
With towers tall and pillars fair
And filled with treasures rich and rare,
And there my fancy free
Dwelt long in ecstasy.

My castle fell but yesterday.
My dreams have vanished quite away.

Upon the sand I wrote a name,
The name of one whose true love came
To set my life in love's sweet frame
Brief picture, fair and sweet
Of happiness, complete.

The name I wrote but yesterday
The morning's tide has wiped away.

I picked a wild rose by the sea,
I thought its beauty bloomed for me,
And took it with me tenderly
Its petals were so fair
Its perfume rich and rare—

The rose I picked but yesterday
I find now fades quite away.

—Abbie Farwell Brown, archived in the
Schlesinger Library at Radcliffe

Revealing glimpses into her dating and social life during these years are seen through the prism of the most self-revealing prose she ever wrote, the fascinating series of articles she wrote for the *St. Louis Globe-Democrat,* under the pseudonym of Jean Neal, during 1898–9. Taken as a whole, they reveal much about women of her time.

In her "Burning Old Letters," it is clear that she has received a lot of letters from men over the years. Of them she observes, "A man . . . never for a moment forgets to whom he is writing. He is conscious of his audience and of himself in relation to it. He does not talk himself out as he would in conversation—where indeed he has the advantage of the average girl in unconscious ease and lack of affectation. But he tries so hard to be adequate. He is not spontaneous; he does not write for the pleasure of it, but only when he has something particular to say is he at his best."

But not always does she find men so self-conscious and stilted: "But when a man who is really worth while forgets his audience and loses his consciousness that he is writing a letter, then indeed are his eagerly scrawled pages worthwhile. Then, when he is genuine and sincere, he is apt also to be more impressive in diction, more forceful in idea and more apt in illustration. I love best of all to correspond with a man on those terms."

In "The Old and the New Valentine," she castigates men for showing so little imagination in their courting: "Men have no imagination nowadays; that's the trouble. . . . It is not the girls' fault that there is so little romance in the world. Indeed, it is they who keep alive what little there is extant; and in their secret souls they mourn because there is no more. . . ."

In "Women and War," written during the Spanish-American War, she notes that "All the world loves a lover, as we know; but from time immemorial all the lassies have loved the soldier laddie. And even though they have no time to look upon us, we watch them off and out of sight with our hearts in our eyes." In "The Summer Man," also written during that war, she resignedly admits that women, when available men are few, so spoil the few men who show up at summer resorts that those men tend to become despots.

In "Picnics and Picnics," she maintains that no more than half of those invited to a picnic should be female; males are essential to the success of such an activity.

"May Day" is a holiday she yearns for as it once was celebrated, but now, she sighs, it has fallen "into disrepute only since men have become too busy and prosaic and commonplace to appreciate it."

But, of them all, she gave herself away most in "Engagement of One's Gentleman Friends." First of all, she labels herself an "immune" (immunity from marrying), declaring, "I think I am an immune myself; at least, no microbe has as yet fixed his cold claw on me—and I have been repeatedly exposed." But then, mixing her signals, she admits that "It is a queer feeling to receive the announcement of an old friend's engagement; queerer still, if once upon a time you might have had the opportunity to write your name in place of that other hers. It has been said, I think, that no woman relishes the idea of losing a devotion once hers to command: still less to see it transferred to another woman. . . . We don't wish it ours again—we could have had it in the first place if we had wanted it. But there certainly is a queer little feeling of pique and almost of jealousy that there should be consolation in the world for the loss of us."

But, she submits, there *are* compensations to singlehood: "Chaperoned by one's juniors, if one happens to have the gift of looking younger than is possible, one can go on, in season and out of season, having the good times which fall only to the lot of bachelor maids. . . . We are envied often, we immunes. . . . Nowadays there is no obloquy attached to the state of spinsterhood—it is quite the fashion to prolong girlhood to the utmost bounds; there is always a chance to change one's mind before it is too late, in case the right one should come along."

Apparently, for her, the right one never did.

A Wandering

The snow-white ships that sail the sea *If only*
Are like adventurous birds, to me.
They spread their wings and fly afar *I*
To foreign lands where wonders are;

Where gondolas ply up and down *could*
The byways of a fairy town;
Where gloomy mountain caverns hold *be*
Forgotten stores of robber gold;
Where tigers in the jungle roam, *a*
And curious creatures are at home;
Where lovely castles gleam in Spain;
Where camels in a winding train *bird*
Bear treasures from Aladdin's land
Across the desert's yellow sand; *and*
Where painted mosques with towers high

Point to the magic eastern sky;
fly.
Where mystic lamps turn night to day;
Where tinkling rainbow fountains play;

Where giants lived, and dragons, too,
Where fairy fancies might come true;
Where everything is quaint and queer,
So different from *now* and *here!*
All tinted amethyst and gold,
And nothing new, but ever old.
Oh
Oh, pennies would be useless there,
But golden sequins are to spare,
my!
And jingling ducats buy such things
As children's dreaming never brings.

Oh, snow-white ships that sail the sea,
Great birds, do lend your wings to me,
And bear me happily some day
To those bright wonders far away!
—Abbie Farwell Brown, "Snow-White Ships," from *A Pocketful of Posies,* 1902

After having dreamed of going abroad for many years, in 1899 Brown made up part of a traveling foursome self-labeled "The Bachelor Girls," and sailed to Europe.

Fortunately, she wrote a series of travel sketches for the *St. Louis Globe-Democrat*; in them is revealed much more of her reactions, impressions, and personality than her trip diary entries do.

"EDINBURGH, SCOTLAND, July 10—It is a bewildering experience for four unsquired dames, little used to traveling, to find themselves stranded in a foreign city . . . with no prospect of finding a lodging for their weary bones [the visit of the Prince of Wales was attracting such crowds that all the available rooms were booked]. At last an angelic maid in the inevitable black gown, white cap and dainty apron of the Scottish chambermaids, gave us faint hope of obtaining an attic room. The quartet fell upon her neck in tearful joy, and accepted any terms, any condition of condensed living—even four in a bed or two in a bath tub was better than renting the cab for the night, as we were desperately contemplating. . . ."

Of the food, she was less than ecstatic: "We cannot get used to the bad coffee, cold bread and meat for breakfast, nor to the overdone beef and uncanny broths at dinner, with the lack of napkins, tea and ice water."

But, oh, the Highland soldier! "Anything more peacocky and dazzling than his six feet of kilt, tartan, bear skin, white coat, gaiters and tattooed knees, would be hard to find. Eh, but he is bonnie and I find my hairt sair taken wi' a' his glory. We saw a regiment of him being drilled at the castle yesterday, and it was like a moving kaleidoscope of color. He is very callous, however, and casts an eye neither to right nor left to notice the admiring lasses who wilt along his path."

The historical sites really meant the most to her. Places like Holyrood Castle:

> We passed into Holyrood with many a tremor of pity for the poor Queen Mary, who seems so specially identified with it. It is a grand place, but very gloomy and sad—not wholly with memories, but because of the architecture of those days and the lack of airy lighting. Mary's apartments, with the little secret stair leading down to Darnley's room, contain many mementos of the ill-fated Queen, and seem full of her presence. Her royal bed, canopied in oak and faded crimson damask, stands close by the door of the little supper room where Rizzio was seized dining with her. The conspirators entered by her secret stair and dragged the poor, beautiful, much-loved youth out at a side door. A sinister spot in the corridor is pointed out as being dyed in his blood. It does no harm to believe the legend unless one is too sensitive to bear the shock which sight of that faint shadow of a stain conveys (excerpted from Jean Neal's [Brown's pseudonym] "Bachelor Girls in Scotland," *St. Louis Globe-Democrat,* July 30, 1899).

Reluctantly leaving Edinburgh, the quartet moved on to Melrose Abbey, Durham, York, Canterbury, Birmingham, Warwick, and Stratford. Then it was on to London, via Kenilworth Castle: "What a joy dear old, smutty, damp, gray London is. . . . Not so strange nor quaint nor grand nor beautiful, perhaps, as what we have seen in many of our wanderings, but every turn of every street brings us up short upon some thrilling site or association: every other corner bears a name which brings our hearts up into our mouths with a queer thump of recognition and greeting. Every little church—and they are thick in London as mosquitoes in New Jersey—has its legend or its sacred shrine of some bookmaking friend, to whom we never come so near in time or place or spirit as now. The very stones beneath one's feet seem to cry out the names of those who have trodden them in times past, and in the thickest whir of traffic one feels the spirit of things which happened long ago."

Everywhere they found memories of Dickens, in "the dirtiest alley in London, Tom All Alone's pathetic graveyard, and in the Old Curiosity Shop."

The brooding Tower of London was quite another story! "The tower filled us with gloom. One could hardly look to enjoy a happy morning in these grim surroundings." In all their many pilgrimages, they did not forget the great British Museum. Above all, they did not forget Westminster Abbey. Three times Brown returned to its Poets' Corner, there to commune and dream.

Not surprisingly, given Brown's love of flowers, she rhapsodized over an endearing trait of Londoners: "We hardly met a man in the morning who had not a posy or boutonniere in his lapel; they always seemed to have time for this little grace, and are not ashamed of being considered effeminate if caught buying flowers on the street. And what delightful flowers they are—how cheap and plentiful! They go by us in little donkey carts heaped high like a huge nosegay, with roses, mignonette, lavender, pinks, violets. Everyone seems fond of them, and everyone seems to consider flowers as one of the actual necessities of life" (excerpted from Brown's "Bachelor Girls in London," *St. Louis Globe-Democrat*, November 19, 1899).

Sadly, the girls bade farewell to London and headed to the Lorna Doone country, Bideford, Salisbury, and the land of Jane Austen; traveling by horse and carriage.

A ship then took them across the windy English Channel to Antwerp and Amsterdam. Germany was next. At Cologne's shrine of St. Ursula and the Eleven Thousand Virgins, Brown came face-to-face with the question: How much is legend and how much is truth? Responding, she admitted, "But we wanted to believe it all—it is really much easier to believe everything than to be a skeptic in the atmosphere of so much obvious age and gorgeous faith; and the chamber was a very holy place to us. . . . And after all, whether the legend be true or no . . . , the sentiment which they have inspired through all these hundreds of years is a touching and beautiful thing, and the floor worn by countless pilgrims' feet, and the cold metal kissed by so many earnest lips, have surely become sacred in their own right."

As for cathedrals and castles, she announced, tongue in cheek, that "If when we reach our native shores we are not able to build for ourselves a cathedral and a ruined castle, it will prove that we are singularly unobservant. I have seen so many of both these specimens of ancient architecture that I feel as if I could make either with both eyes shut. After climbing to the top of Cologne Cathedral, the second tallest building in the world, I believe, oh, how my legs did ache! And after a glorious day on the Rhine, whisking by countless castles of every pattern and variety, to say nothing of a special visit to Heidelberg Castle, with careful inspection of every dungeon and battlement, I feel that I have acquired the cathedral-castle recipe. But I won't give it away. It's too precious" (excerpted from Brown's "Bachelor Girls in Kaiser William's Country," *St. Louis Globe-Democrat*, October 8, 1899).

Switzerland and the Alps were next. Hordes of Cookies (tourists led by Cook guides) were everywhere, each with chamois beard and edelweiss-bedecked-hat and notched alpenstock cane, induced them to sing a popular tourist ditty often:

"I would not be a Cookie,
Nor with the Cookies stand,
The edelweiss on my forehead,
An alpenstock in my hand."

Not that they hadn't tried to fit in, but their alpenstocks were "continually poking into the eyes of porters and of drivers and fellow travelers, and (worst of all) of us." Besides that, they were always being left somewhere. Oh yes, and making them the laughingstock of whoever was around. So they were not at all brokenhearted when a porter walked away with the alpenstocks in Geneva, and never brought them back.

But, never to be forgotten was Zermatt and the Matterhorn. " . . . ah, what a glorious day that was—my birthday—and spent in a heavenly meadow, pink with alpine lilies in the shadow of that great sky-biting tooth. My birthday cake was a plummy mountain frosted with snow; the loveliest of alpine flowers in countless varieties garlanded the feast, and a brilliant peak, one for each year of my life, stood up for candles all about. It was the best birthday party I ever had. . . ."

In those days, travel in the mountains was not for the faint of heart. They traveled in horse-drawn diligences ("like open victorias, with an extra seat above behind the driver"). "Our road to Chamonix over the famous Tete Noir Pass is a ticklish experience for weak nerves. . . . Such dizzy precipices sheering down into gorges of jagged, hard rock, with rushing torrents at the bottom. We would go under an arch of rock, through a black hole of a tunnel, and emerge to find the horses' hoofs clinging to the very edge of the cliff, at a right-angle of the road" (excerpted from Brown's "Bachelor Girls in the Alps," *St. Louis Globe-Democrat,* October 22, 1899).

Then it was Paris! The shopping was both wonderful and addictive. But, as to the cabmen ". . . who take basest advantage of our not being able to argue in voluble French. Of all misguided and gallows-bound rogues the French cabman is the most to be anathematized. We found his species civil in England, bland in Belgium, dull in Holland, obstinate in Germany, and guileful in Switzerland. But in Paris he is villainy itself. Not only does he unmercifully beat his horse as I have never seen horses abused elsewhere, not only does he drive so carelessly that the wheels of your cabriolet are forever becoming entangled with the other cabs which pass in the night, not only does he smoke bad cigars whose smoke puffs into your face, and swears horrid French, swears at every one he encounters—but he charges you for overtime and weeps if you refuse his unrighteous demands. And of all unendurable horrors a weeping thief is the worst. . . ."

As to the city itself, "You can't tell what may happen in Paris at any minute, we have this feeling continually in this joyous, reckless, clean and sparkling city, which has bathed in blood so often. Everything looks new and fresh as if just made; and the most cheerful places of all are the sights of wholesale murders and awful crimes" (excerpted from "Bachelor Girls in Paris," *St. Louis Globe-Democrat,* November 5, 1899).

Finally, exhausted from the unrelenting pace of their sightseeing, they crossed the Channel to England. Windsor Castle, where Queen Victoria resided, was their last destination. Brown climbed high up into the castle tower; far away, she could see Eton College and the spire of Stoke Pogis Church, "where 'Elegy in a Country Churchyard' was born and where Gray lies buried." She wrapped up her life-changing trip with these words: "It makes one feel queer to stand by the grave of Kings. One cannot help feeling a little sense of triumph in one's life and power and youth, realizing how much better it is to be a live dog than a dead lion.

"For, is it not far more satisfactory to be looking forward to a joyous sea trip to good old America, with a turkey dinner and jolly American cooking at its end, than to be lying there in royal state, shorn of one's head, or with a bullet through one's heart, amid all the pride, pomp and circumstance of knightly gear and golden shields and rampant lions?

"And now to pack my trunk." (excerpted from "Bachelor Girls at Windsor Castle," *St. Louis Globe-Democrat*, December 3, 1899; other references are from Brown's trip journal, archived in the Schlesinger Library of Radcliffe).

Little Brothers

Like Hiawatha.

I wish I knew the simple words
To talk with Fish and Beasts and Birds!
We call them "dumb" because they speak
A tongue not English, French, or Greek;

Animals are not dumb!

But they are wiser far than we,
And often grieve, it seems to me,
Because we folk of Tailor-Land
Can't answer them nor understand.

We are dull.

How pleasant it would be to stray
About the woods and fields all day,
Conversing with them, high and low,
Of matters that one wants to know.

Tree-top tales.

I should learn very curious things
From Brother Bird who loaned his wings
To bear me up into the sky,
Till never child had soared so high!

Water-wonders.

And Brother Fish would teach the maze
Of ripple-paths and water-ways;

Would tell me fishy tales, and show
What fishermen can never know.

Four-footed fun.

Then Brother Beasts would make me wise
With secrets which a man would prize.
The bigger Beasts would walk beside,

Big eyes! And bear me when I chose to ride;
Big teeth! They would defend me from the foe,
Red tongues! And teach the safest way to go.
The little ones would find me food,
And bring me news of bad and good;
And I should love them, oh! so well,
But kind And they would know, for I could tell.
to me. So I should be their little King,
To share their life in everything.

All this I cannot do, indeed;
But it is 'most as good to read,
I shall All cuddled in some cosy nook,
play Of Mowgli in the Jungle Book;
Mowgli. Of Mowgli who, it seems to me,
Is what one most would like to be!

—Abbie Farwell Brown, from *A Pocketful of Posies*, 1902)

The twenty-eight-year-old dreamer who returned home to Boston on the eve of a new century was not at all the same person who had left five months before. Before, she had only read about these things in books, now she had seen and experienced them first-hand: castles and cathedrals, dungeons and gardens, knightly armor and blood-stained axe, the "Venus de Milo" and the "Mona Lisa." In Europe, legend perceived as truth had forced her to reevaluate what was real and what was not.

Only a little over a month after her ship carried her home in time for Thanksgiving, midnight bells rang in a new century. And fourteen months later, January 22, 1901, Victoria, empress of a quarter of mankind, was dead. She had come to the throne way back in 1837, and had mourned her husband Albert's death for forty long years.

On the streets of America, most of the world's automobiles—some 8,000—competed with some ten million bicycles and eighteen million horses and mules. The world, it was changing.

But Miss Brown was not much concerned with the technology of this new age: the automobile, the ever-faster trains, the airplane, each resulting in an ever-faster pace of life. Ideas generated by the long trip whirled relentlessly in her head, giving her no peace until they were dealt with.

First and foremost was her first book with Houghton Mifflin, *The Book of Saints and Friendly Beasts* (1900), inspired by what she discovered in England's Chester Cathedral: Carved in its choir stalls were scenes depicting the life of St. Werburg. Obviously, the product of meticulous and extensive research, within the book's covers she explored the symbiotic relationship between certain men, women, and the animal world, starting way back with St. Francis who knew that "all the creatures are our little brothers, ready to meet half way those who will but try to understand."

All of these stories deal with men and women, boys and girls, who, at least according to legend, had both the inclination and the ability to reach across the communication chasm which normally separates man from animal, human from non-human.

No book Brown ever wrote has proven more popular than this; even today, Brown aficionados diligently seek it out.

However, another of Brown's books which has exercised the same staying power (at least in the used book market) as its illustrious predecessor: *The Lonesomest Doll* (1902), the story of a friendship between a sheltered child queen (Clothilde) and a gatekeeper's daughter (Nichelte). The catalyst is a doll so beautiful and so valuable that she is neither played with or loved. So popular has it been, in fact, that several decades later, it was reissued, featuring Arthur Rackham illustrations.

A Pocketful of Posies (1902) and *Fresh Posies* (1908) featured the best of Brown's early poetry, especially those written primarily for children.

Another powerful book for young people was her *In the Days of Giants: A Book of Norse Tales* (1902), in which she retells fascinating Scandinavian myths. Altogether, a deeply moving book about the Norse gods, Brown telling each story simply, movingly, and beautifully. It reads like the Fall of Eden or Camelot, with Loki, the scheming Lucifer or the plotting Mordred, who brought sorrow and darkness to the world—and an end to joyous Vahhalla. Balder, the Norse Prometheus or Christ figure, was beloved by C. S. Lewis, who borrowed more from Norse mythology than from any other. So splendidly written is this book that it remained a standard on children's library shelves several generations after it was first published.

The Curious Book of Birds (1903) humanizes birds, much as does Kipling in his *Jungle Book* and Thornton Burgess in his beloved stories. Brown ranged far in seeking out folk stories: some from the ancient world (mostly European), some from the Orient, some from Africa, and some from Native American lore.

The Flower Princess (1904) is actually a quartet of stories. "The Flower Princess," the story of a beautiful princess who determines to marry only someone who loves flowers as much as she does (unquestionably, one could validly substitute Abbie Farwell Brown as the Princess and not lose a nuance, so great was her personal love for flowers); "The Little Friend," a Christmas "inasmuch" story, was later published as a separate book; "The Mermaid's Child" is a Cain and Abel type narrative, with a humanized "mer-child" sacrificed by a jealous brother. Interestingly enough, a stork acts as the all-seeing mediator and judge in the story. "The Ten Blowers" is the supreme example of farcical slapstick humor in Brown's canon. Altogether, a remarkable book!

Next came two related books: *Brothers and Sisters* (1906), and *Friends and Cousins* (1907). In the first book, many of the stories feature the same children, and each story intertwines action, suspense, and Judeo-Christian values. Some of the stories take place in a child's fairyland world and some of them take place on a very real island off the Maine coast. So popular were the Maine island stories that Brown brought the protagonists back again in *Friends and Cousins*. The dominant theme in all the stories is integrity—not in a preachy sense but in an undergirding sense.

John of the Woods (1909) is a wonderful adaptation spinning off from *The Book of Saints and Friendly Beasts*. The hero, John, is a battered orphan boy who flees his tormenters by escaping into the Italian forests. His life is saved by John the Hermit, a St. Francis-type whom all the animals and birds of the forest love. After John matures, the sanctuary of the forest is desecrated by a hunting king and prince, determined to slay at will. From that moment on, the idyl ceases and suspense sets in. It is thereafter virtually un-put-downable! In a very special sense, this is a premodern, pro-environment book, preaching the interconnectedness of all life and the need to protect all of God's creatures.

The Christmas Angel (1910) was, of course, her first great Christmas book.

With these almost yearly books taking much of her time, Brown still managed to find time to write a steady stream of poetry, short stories, and plays. According to Jo Ann Abraham Reiss, "she had a special gift for writing poetry appropriate to a musical setting, and for years was commissioned by Silver, Burdett & Company to contribute lyrics for songs in their Progressive Music Series. Collaborating with the composer Mabel W. Daniels, she won a Girl Scout competition for 'On the Trail,' which was adopted as the official song of the Girl Scouts." Beginning in 1902, she somehow also found time to serve as an editor of the "Young Folks Library," a twenty volume series published by Hall & Locke, as well as return to Europe again and again. (Reiss sketch is archived in the Schlesinger Library of Radcliffe.)

She was fortunate in that she wrote and published during what is called the Golden Age of Children's Literature. But the tradition she represents best can be traced back through Howard Pyle, Andrew Lang, Nathaniel Hawthorne, Washington Irving, the Brothers Grimm, and Hans Christian Andersen, authors who reinterpreted mythology and legends especially for children.

The Inkwell

My bottle of ink once said to me —
"Did you but know, could you but see
The wonderful stories all distilled
With which my inkiness is filled.

They are swimming around, a million words
To tell of fanciful beasts and birds,
Fairies, pirates, girls and boys,
Treasure ships and beautiful toys.

You go fishing around with a pen
Catching a little tale now and then
But there they lurk, a million more,
That nobody ever caught before."

Then I shook that ink and stirred it well,
I fished. And what do you think befell?
A wee little minnow was all that bit,
But I hauled him out. And this is it.

—Abbie Farwell Brown, archived in the
Schlesinger Library at Radcliffe

The years continued to sweep by, and the "golden-haired, petite [she was only 5'3"], piquant-faced little authoress" kept mighty busy. ("Peace With a Sword," February 1918 news clipping is archived in the Schlesinger Library of Radcliffe.)

It was during this second decade of the new century that Brown grew more reflective, perhaps sensing she might not live a long life.

She became more concerned about her legacy—not merely her poems, short stories, plays, lyrics, and books, but her insights into the world children live in, and the role the written and spoken word ought to play in their lives. Not only did she write about these two areas of intense concern, but she lectured all over the country about them as well.

Four lectures had to do with "The Child and the Book." In them, she maintained that growth in spirituality, imagination, empathy and taste was best achieved indirectly, through books, agreeing completely with Tennyson.

"For truth in closest words shall fail,
When truth embodied in a tale
Shall enter in at lowly doors!"
(from *In Memorium)*

Preschoolers. Her first talk had to do with children ages one through four. Her first concern had to do with the overall atmosphere of the home: "Books are the heart of the house—keep them lying about. The living room ought to be the book room, but even in the nursery there ought to be a book shelf. The overriding goal during these crucial first four years ought to be to make a book-lover of the child, and to develop the child's vocabulary."

The Story Hour she considered supremely important, and emphasized telling stories, reading stories aloud, cozy book-reading corners, bedtime stories, the impact of regular habit in this respect, and the long-term impact of story-related memories.

As for the physical book, she urged parents to inculcate reverence for it, to teach children to be careful in their book-handling, to encourage curiosity, to not cheapen books by too great numbers of them, and to teach them how books are made. Her list of no-no-nevers consisted of these: Don't buy for small children books that are (1) ugly, (2) poorly printed, (3) poorly bound, (4) inadequately illustrated, (5) incorporate overly shiny paper, (6) are too heavy.

Children Ages Four to Seven. Action is more important now. Boys and girls are still alike interest-wise. This is not an age for children to tell the stories, but for parents to. During this age, their sense of right and wrong is rapidly developing, as is the conscience. Emphasize manners, kindness, generosity, sympathy, empathy, and truthfulness. Curiosity is being awakened, and they'll have *lots* of questions. They are ready for true stories and facts of nature, and imagination-development, but it is important to discriminate between facts and imagination. This is an excellent age for fairy tales, fables, myths, legends, heroes, lessons of good and evil, simple truths of life, justice, retribution. Brown points out that "nature and fairy lore are not incompatible; love of fairy world being the beginning of imagination in the child."

In poetry, you should now move from the simple to poetry with a meaning. In religious works, read the Scriptures aloud so as to communicate beauty of words; also read from *Pilgrim's Progress* and from legends of saints and good people. Be morally indirect rather than too preachy.

Children Ages Seven to Twelve. Major changes occur during these years. They are now of school age. The imagination really flowers during this period! Areas to be emphasized include conscience, social virtues, curiosity, precepts, and imagination. Interest-wise, boys and girls now begin to diverge. There should be twofold development: spiritual and practical. They are beginning to react as they observe, are sensitive to suggestions, and are increasingly self-conscious. They have a growing antipathy to overt moralizing, desiring instead *Deeds, not words!* In reading, they are intrigued by slang, and increasingly enjoy shocking by choice of words.

Their individuality is continuing to flower: *Feed the strongest interest!* Since this is the age of hero worship (especially for boys), feed them stories of chivalry, adventure, clan-spirit, pirates, and secrecy. Girls, on the other hand, are growing more responsible and sentimental and can be over-conscientious. They are ready for brave girls and gentle boys (Joan of Arc, Galahad). Thus boys and girls need to be addressed differently now, but encourage sympathy and empathy so they don't despise or put down the other. A good age for historic girls' and historic boys' series. Both the ideal and the practical need to be emphasized, especially the love of beauty, strength, and nobility.

Important to be reading the Bible out loud, as well as religious magazines; emphasize Bible heroes and saintly individuals. The best way to internalize chivalry, bravery, sacrifice, loyalty, and devotion, however, is through romances.

Poetry-wise, *there is no danger of too much!* Building on Field and Riley, stir in Whittier, Arnold, Robin Hood-type ballads, Longfellow (especially

Hiawatha), Tennyson, Holmes (the humorous ones), Shakespeare (retold); same for Chaucer. *Soak the modern child with poetry!*

Brown, quoting from *St. Nicholas Magazine*, sums up this section in these words:

> *If they have good taste and good*
> *moral standards at age twelve—they*
> *will not be easily lost.*

Boys and Girls Ages Twelve to Sixteen. During these years, they continue to develop a sense of responsibility; and their ability to think and reason is strengthened. It is an age of *doing*. A sense of individuality becomes obvious. It is time to encourage honesty, loyalty, and generosity in girls, and kindness, delicacy, tact, and self-sacrifice in boys. Boys of this age love the sturdy virtues of danger, strength, pirates, secrecy, clan-spirit, and athletic books. They tend to gravitate toward objective things. Girls, on the other hand, tend to gravitate toward the sentimental, romantic, morbid, introspective, and the subjective. Again, *girls will read the boys' books—not vice-versa.* They share a common love of romance and adventure, but boys are fascinated by the practical and hate sentiment, whereas the girls are more dreamy.

This is a crucial age for developing standards of life, behavior, *character*. Introducing them to good biography is crucial at this age. History and travel broadens their interests, and citizenship can be inculcated through books like *Man Without a Country*.

It is extremely important that poetry not be neglected during this age. They are ready for heavier things now—*The Great Ones!* Avoid edited, condensed versions—*they are not very real*—and *stick to the complete text.*

Brown summed up this section with this statement: "Classics are read before thirteen—or never" (excerpted from "The Child and the Book" lecture notes, archived in the Schlesinger Library of Radcliffe).

Brown also lectured on the subject of poetry. First of all, she noted that poetry is ruined for many children because of adult emphasis on artificiality in elocution ("imitation, rather than imagination"). All art requires imagination. Make poetry fun, such as she did in "The Candy Lion":

Harmless	A CANDY Lion's very good
and	Because he cannot bite,
sweet-	Nor wander roaring for his food,
tempered	Nor eat up folks at night.

But though it's very nice for me,
It's not so nice for him;
For every day he seems to be
More shapeless and more slim.

Fades away somehow

And first, there's no tail any more;
And next, he has no head;
And then,—he's just a candy Roar,
And might as well be dead.

Why! Why!

So, You *eat* Him *up*

—Abbie Farwell Brown,
from *Pocketful of Posies,* 1902

A writer who can make poetry fun for children is special indeed—but one who can be informative and educational without losing the impishness and whimsy . . . is a *master!* Note her poem "The Spoiled Violin," in this respect:

I know a little family,
A family of Strings;
Viol is their ancient name, —
They are the quaintest things!

Viol Family.

Their family resemblances
Are very, very strong,
They haven't any hands nor feet,
But oh, their necks are long!

Good voices, too.

Bass Viol is the big Papa,
Who stands against the wall;
And Mother 'Cello, soft and sweet,
Near by, is 'most as tall.

Papa and Mamma.

Next there is sister Viola
(Who used to be a twin),
But crowding in before them all
Is little Violin.

Sister and little Brother.

Mamma has often said to me —
I'm sure of every word —
That when the grown-up people speak,
I must be seen, not *heard.*

Seen, not not heard.

But in the family of Strings
It is not so at all,
For Father only mumbles things
Up there against the wall;

"Gr-r-r!" growls Bass Viol.

And Mother 'Cello's voice is low,
And Viola's is thin,
But always louder than the rest
Talks little Violin.

"Tum-te-dum!" "Teedle-dee!" "P-r-r-r, squeak-squeak! Tra-la-la-oh!"

He interrupts them when he likes;
They cannot keep him still.
He runs and quavers, laughs and whines;
His voice is high and shrill.

"Tra-la-la-oh, squeak-squeak! Pr-r-r-r, zim, zim, zim!"

No matter who was speaking first,
No matter what they play,
The Violin just pitches in
And always has his say.

Rude boy!

If I were Violin's Papa, —
Bass Viol, six feet high, —
I would not let my silly son
Think he was big as I.

I'd spank him,

If I were Mrs. 'Cello, too,
I'd bring him up to be
A nice, well-mannered Violin,
Seen and not heard—like me.

wouldn't you?

—Abbie Farwell Brown, from
A Pocketful of Posies, 1902

As for her books published during the second decade of the century, her second Christmas book, *Their City Christmas,* was published in 1912. While it is a good book, it lacks the power of *The Christmas Angel.* The story is about a fisherman's family on a Maine island and their relationship to the affluent family that vacations in Maine during the summer, but lives in Boston the rest of the time; now, at Christmas, the city children invite the island twins to

Boston for the Christmas holidays. Homely values permeate the story.

The Lucky Stone (1914) is a wondrous book! The plot has to do with a delightful orphan named Maggie who yearns for love, beauty, and the opportunity to escape the ugly world of tenements for the outdoors; a beautiful "princess" who has everything money can buy but is bored and lonely; a teacher-social worker who befriends Maggie and longs for serenity and an unarticulated dream woman. The catalyst is "The Lucky Stone." It is a book to fall in love with!

Kisington Town (1915) is unlike any book I ever met—based on a rather wild premise that there could be a city-state where all the *really* important people are affiliated with the city library! Well, an evil tyrant, Red Rex, attacks the city, and its destruction appears certain. The only person who can possibly save it is the boy Harold, who just happens to be a master storyteller, of the caliber of Scheherazade of *Arabian Nights.*

Rock of Liberty (1918) is a patriotic cantata based on a poem she wrote titled "Peace With a Sword." She wrote it to generate patriotism and encourage young men and women to volunteer to help beat back the "barbarians" in World War I. A year earlier, the work had been set to music and performed by Boston's Handel and Haydn Society.

Heart of New England (1920) is a remarkable tribute to the tough hardscrabble world of her ancestors, New England. It is her most patriotic book. Brown strongly empathized with the true unsung heroes in New England history: the women who suffered so much but received so little credit for it. "Pilgrim Mothers," the fourth poem in the collection, is one of the finest and most moving poems she ever wrote:

> Now thank God for the women
>   Who dared the perilous sea
> With our adventurous ancestors,
>   To bear them company!
>
> They sailed, they knew not whither,
>   They came, nor questioned why,
> But that the men-folk whom they loved
>   Without their care would die.
>
> Babies newly born they carried,
>   And bairns with wavering feet;

But never a cow was there for milk,
And never a stove for heat.

Through icy waves they landed,
They washed in frozen streams;
They shivered through the nights of dread
With horror in their dreams.

Through toil and want and danger
High-hearted they could wait;
They lived and died for the commonweal,
And mothered a nursling State.

They had no voice in meeting,
No vote in pact or law;
But of their flesh and blood is built
Our strength for peace and war.

Thank God for the brave women
Of a hard three-hundred years!
Have they not earned a nation's trust
Through sacrifice and tears?
—Abbie Farwell Brown, from *Heart of New England*, 1920

Under the Rowan Tree (1926) is an anthology of eighteen loosely related stories written at various stages of Brown's career. Unfortunately, the collection lacks cohesiveness and focus.

We are still searching for copies of a number of her books, so they can be evaluated and described. They are: *Notable Trees about Boston* (1900), *The Curious Book of Birds* (1903), *The Star Jewels and Other Wonders* (1905), *Tales of the Red Children* (1909), *The Boy Mozart* (1910), *Songs of Sixpence* (1914), *Surprise House* (1917), *Round Robin* (1921), and *The Lights of Beacon Hill* (1922).

Meanwhile, her stories, poetry, and plays continued to be published by the nation's major magazines, and her name recognition continued to grow.

The Silver Stair

I traveled by the path of Pain
  Unto the gate of Day
But Love has besought me back again
  So I retraced my way.

To live and love and labor still
  And finish it may be
Some special task my Father's will
  Has set aside for me.
    —Abbie Farwell Brown, "The Traveler Returned," archived in the Schlesinger Library at Radcliffe

The Great War was at last over, the boys had come home—except for the thousands buried under white crosses "over there." Prosperity came sweeping back, and America entered a new age, acclaimed as the savior of Europe.

But there in the venerable Brown home on Beacon Hill, life went on pretty much as usual. The pattern of her life now established, its images and colors clear, her days and nights settled into a fairly predictable routine. She exercised vigorously, playing tennis and golf, walked a great deal, bicycled, and danced. She loved to put on (and attend) parties of all kinds, be they advertising parties, valentine parties, ghost parties, dramatic vignettes from life parties, or just-because parties. Picnics with the right company were always a joy. And how she loved to travel, to wander abroad, and then to wander home. In fact, she labeled traveling as the only sure cure for weather-induced blues. "Of course, some more than others are slaves to the whims of the sun, rain and wind. I confess to being that most sensitive of unpractical scientific instruments, the human barometer. As the sun smiles, so do I. When it rains I am like the 'sorry little pig.' With mouth drawn down at the corners and with a hatred of my fellow man in my bosom. On these days life is not popular with me, and my spirits sink way down below freezing point into the bulb of despair." But, even during such dismal days, just the thought of travel was enough to unwilt her leaves (excerpted from Brown's "A Sure Cure for the Blues," *St. Louis Globe-Democrat*, January 29, 1899).

But lest we be left with too gloomy a picture of her, normally she was the most joyful of human beings. In fact, she submitted that every day ought to be celebrated as an anniversary of something, not just the usual national holidays. In "Anniversaries That Thrill," she raved about "What a kaleidoscopic variety of color is offered by a whole year of days, no two alike, each one famous for some event of time, remote or near." Perhaps it might be an anniversary of a famous battle that changed the course of history. "How near it brings us to history, to the people who lived and fought and died those many years ago, when we think that upon a morning, very like this, mayhap, so many people opened their eyes all unknowing on a day which was to make a milestone in the world's annals—and at night of that same day so many eyes were closed to open no more."

But, almost as thrilling to her, was to open her eyes and greet an anniversary having to do with a favorite author. Then there are the many festivals of the church. "Each is a day of days, distinct, replete with tradition, romance, legend, literature and fancy; that each brings to mind its own vivid pictures, its own wealth of suggestion and its own charm for the ensuing hours. . . . We will scatter fern seed on St. John's Eve, and become invisible, so that we can see the fairies' pranks unobserved. We will go a-Maying, and also note before that on April 19 it is Primrose Day, and we must wear the yellow dainties, playing we are in England. We will eat goose at Michaelmas and hot cross buns on Good Friday, and we will observe the saints' days, each in its due time, for many of the legends are very beautiful, and it is well to know them."

In her case, of course, she has jotted down the birth dates of family or friends—but far more importantly, she has filled her book with anniversaries of writers, musicians, painters, anyone who beautified the earth. When the natal day of a great writer arrives, she greets it with one of his or her quotations. In short, Brown maintains that, with such daily riches at hand, it ought to be impossible to become blasé or disillusioned (excerpted from Brown's "Anniversaries That Thrill," *St. Louis Globe-Democrat*, March 5, 1899).

While she loved the serenity of the countryside, the mountains, rivers, and seas, she was also very much a city woman, reveling in its amenities, its concerts, its plays, its lectures, its art exhibits, its formal dining, its sidewalk cafes, its opportunities to participate in great events.

Not the least of her many contributions had to do with her untiring leadership roles within the New England literary community. Not only was she an active member of the Boston Authors' Club, the Boston Drama League, and the Poetry Society of America, she was also a charter member of the New England Poetry Club—in fact it had been organized at her home in 1915, and she was serving as its president at the time of her death in 1927 (Reiss, 249).

Caroline Ticknor, author, editor, and playwright, member of one of New England's most illustrious publishing families, and one of Brown's closest friends, categorized her a "Poet and Friend; or rather one should say Friend and Poet, so vital was her contribution in the field of sympathy and friendship. Wherever she touched other lives she gave herself so generously and freely, that what she was, almost obscured the many things that she did. Yet her accomplishments were manifold, and she excelled in all that she attempted. Her books of prose and verse, her work upon the platform, her clubs, her college, her church, her country, to each she gave unstintingly its rightful share of her well-balanced life, discharging each responsibility with equal zeal, and doing everything with her whole heart. Yet, while she gave ungrudgingly to many interests, she was above all else a poet, whose exquisite productions placed her in the front ranks of our American poets.

"Especially will her sprightly and sparkling verses for little people remain a never-failing source of joy to the young readers, singing straight from her heart into their own, brimming with fun and frolic, sweet, wholesome, and inspiring, she speaks with the authority of one who knows the fairies and understands the language of the 'little brothers' of the animal creation. So truly was she at home in fairyland and elfland that she might well have been herself the Queen of the Fairies, or an imprisoned Dryad. One cannot read her poem 'Sylvia' without instant assurance that there she flashed a searchlight upon herself:

Sylvia is always gay,
When she winged to earth one day,
Through the wonders of the sky,
She caught a star as she flew by,
Green and gold and amethyst,
In her tiny baby fist,
And hid it in her little breast
As a secret unconfessed.

Like a jeweled lantern she
Shines for all the world to see,
In her eyes the sparkle beams,
From her burnished hair it gleams;
Radiant all she does and says,
All her pretty, twinkling ways —
Just because she dared to leaven
Lifetime with a bit of heaven,
Sylvia! Without your spark
Oh, the journey would be dark.

—Abbie Farwell Brown, archived in the Schlesinger Library at Radcliffe (Ticknor, March 23, 1927)

In 1924, her tribute to America's first great composer, *The Boyhood of Edward MacDowell* (who had lived close to the Brown home), was published. She subtitled it "A Boy Who Never Grew Up." Concentrating on his Quaker childhood and youthful study in Europe, rather than adult traumas, still she managed to bring his memorable life story full circle. It is a moving tribute to a great man!

The Silver Stair (1926) was destined to be the last book she saw through to completion. Reading the poems in the collection it is clear she sensed the tides of her life were running back out to that greater sea. There is much here about the ocean, autumn, and old age—and little here for children. It seems obvious that she knew her pixie grace was gone forever, that God was calling her home, for her *joie de vivre* is noticeably in short supply—and all that was left was the putting out to sea with the withdrawing tide, and the darkening west.

The Lantern and Other Plays for Children (1928) was published posthumously. In it are four plays: *The Lantern*, a play set during the American Revolution, with the heroic role carried by the child Barbara. *Rhoecus* is a haunting poem involving Rhoecus, lover of the woods who tries to keep a five-hundred-year-old monarch of the forest from being chopped down; Chloe, the rather insensitive daughter of the determined woodsman; and the tormented Dryad, forced to make a life-changing decision. *The Wishing Moon* has to do with children seeking extraordinary powers on St. John's Eve; and *The Little Shadows* is a dramatized version of Stevenson's shadow poem. It is a splendid collection! The fact that it was republished half a century later testifies to the enduring qualities of these plays.

Very little is said about the role of her father in her life; clearly, he was a man of business, concentrating his considerable energies in the family company which dealt with whale oil and candles. But her mother was the guiding beacon of her life, and enjoyed a long life. Abbie would dedicate *The Silver Stair* collection to her mother, bringing her life and career full circle back to the woman who gave birth to it all.

No doubt the daughter assumed her mother's longevity would be her heritage as well, but alas! It was not to be. It came suddenly, out of a cloudless sky, to this daughter of New England, this lover of life in all its many dimensions.

It seemed she was just entering into the flood-tide of her fame and influence. Carolyn Ticknor noted that, "Those who were present at that triumphal gathering, a few months since, where to a host of friends she read selections from her latest book, *The Silver Stair*, will not forget the warmth of the ovation tendered by that enthusiastic audience composed of personal friends and lovers of her books.

"And to the poet it was a joyful climax to her years of steadily ascending literary achievement. Serene, lovely, and glad almost to tears, the title of her book, *The Silver Stair*, seemed to mark the ascent on which she paused prepared for further flight" (Ticknor, March 23, 1927).

The title of this last book was taken from one of Brown's most powerful poems, about twin sisters, one born with a longing for the hills and the other one for the sea. Brown had used the image earlier in her wondrous story, "The Mermaid Necklace," twenty years before. In that story, written during the morning of her life, the Silver Stair was a resplendent ladder, connecting sea to sky.

Hardly had the glow of her triumph faded when the terrible blow landed: She who had always reveled in the visual, approaching each dawn with the joy of a child, was going *blind!* How could she possibly face a life devoid of light? The answer was not long in coming:

In the Dark

In the dark I lie and think
Of the glory in a day;
Of the sunshine and the shade,
All the color, soft or gay.

I can see it better now
As I lie with curtained eyes.

Oh, the rainbow and the moon:
Oh, the opal of the skies!

How the poppies glow and thrill,
How the pigeon-feathers shine!
I will weave them into dreams,
I will make them ever mine.

All the wonder of a wave,
All the magic of a tree,
I shall wear them in my soul
When these eyes no longer see.

—Abbie Farwell Brown, from
Heart of New England, 1920

The rest of the story was chronicled movingly, and with a broken heart, by her friend: "Out of the threatening dark she emerged hopefully, ready to meet the issue undaunted, ready to follow the gleaming of that inner torch, which should shed life upon her interrupted work.

"And then the second summons sounded, to lay aside that work. . . . With equal courage she faced the final edict which called her to the conflict with pain and mortal illness, and bade her lay aside her pen, even when life seemed sweetest, and most full of opportunity. With fortitude and faith she met this final test, hopefully, prayerfully, still trusting the beneficence of the Eternal One, her guiding star.

"And so she climbed the 'Silver Stair' and vanished from our sight, to live forever in our hearts" (Ticknor, March 23, 1927).

The last poem in *The Silver Stair* is one that must have raised eyebrows when it was published—after all, she was only 55. Did she know something, or sense something, her readers didn't know? It almost seems so:

The Book of Me

I do not know the history that lies
Beyond the present page; I may not peer
Further than where one sets the marker here,
At this day's chapter. Not with childish eyes
Shall I anticipate the next surprise,
Nor flutter through the leaves in hope or fear,

To learn the story's end, however near,
And foil the Author's loving mysteries.

There may be pain, unbearable if guessed
Through waiting hours; but soon forgotten, blent
Into the plot whereby I live and look.
There must be joy—no story so unblessed
As to miss that. I trust and am content;
Until a solemn *Finis* ends the book.

—Abbie Farwell Brown, from *The Silver Stair*, 1926

Typical of letters pouring in to the family after her swift passing is this one from friend and Boston luminary Vida O. Scudder: "We who love radiant Abbie mourn with you; why, the whole city mourns with you, I think. I do not know any one whose loss would be so generally felt; her sweet wholesomeness, her vital charm, her inexhaustible sympathies, endeared her everywhere and illumined every circle in which she moved—I suppose even in paradise it was felt that Abbie was needed so much that she must be called there!" (letter to Ethel Brown, archived in the Schlesinger Library of Radcliffe).

- - -

Joseph Leininger Wheeler, Ph.D.
The Grey House
Conifer, Colorado

The Works of Abbie Farwell Brown

Magazines

This magazine listing is very incomplete; consequently, I am hoping collectors of Abbie Farwell Brown will fill me in with copies of missing entries so we can update our readers in future printings.

1891 "A Topsy-Turvy Piece," *Woman's Home Companion*, September

1892 "A Clover," *Harvard Advocate*, May 18

1893 "Luck" (poem), *New England Magazine*, November

1894 "The Burying of the Hatchet," *New England Magazine*, July
"Valentine: Sweet, Has the Snowdrop Blossomed?" (poem), *New England Magazine*, March

1895 "Haunted House" (poem), *New England Magazine*, May
"A New Evening's Entertainment," *Ladies' Home Journal*, January (illustrated by Charles Gibson)
"For an Evening Party—The Advertising Game," *Ladies' Home Companion*, April 15
"A Dish of Tea," *Peterson's Magazine*, August
"A Ghost Party," *Ladies' Home Companion*, October 1

1896 "Love's Calendar" (poem), *New England Magazine*, March
"Valentine: If Twere Spring" (poem), *New England Magazine*, March
"As Luck Would Have It," *The Housewife*, June
"When Churchyards Yawn," *Boston Post*, September 15

1897 "A Valentine Party," *Woman's Home Companion*, February
"New England Valentine" (poem), *New England Magazine*, February
"The Indian Spring" (poem), *New England Magazine*, June
"Indian Pipes" (poem), *New England Magazine*, August
"His Adopted Friend," *Woman's Home Companion*, September
"In the Fog," *The Housewife*, September
"Rosemary" (poem), *New England Magazine*, November
"A Christmas Gift," *Woman's Home Companion*, December

1898 "His Freshman Romance," *Woman's Home Companion*, January
"Moods" (poem), *New England Magazine*, January
"Burning Old Letters" (Jean Neal, pseudonym), *St. Louis Globe-Democrat*, January 23
"A Defense of the Tea Habit" (Jean Neal, pseudonym), *St. Louis Globe-Democrat*, January 30
"The Old and New Valentine" (Jean Neal, pseudonym), *St. Louis Globe-Democrat*, February 13
"Women's Clubs" (Jean Neal, pseudonym), *St. Louis Globe-Democrat*, February 20
"A Home Run," *Vogue*, March 17
"I Did Not Know" (poem), *New England Magazine*, April

"The Modern Girl and Athletics" (Jean Neal, pseudonym), *St. Louis Globe-Democrat*, April 11
"Pastoral" (poem), *New England Magazine*, May
"A Painted Conscience," *St. Louis Globe-Democrat,* May 1
"A Defense of the Diary" (Jean Neal, pseudonym), *St. Louis Globe-Democrat*, May 22
"The Minions of Fashion" (Jean Neal, pseudonym), *St. Louis Globe-Democrat*, May 29
"The Tour of the Four," *The Ladies' World*, June
"Tryst" (poem), *New England Magazine*, July
"From Sandal to Shoe" (Jean Neal, pseudonym), *St. Louis Globe-Democrat*, July 3
"Women and the War" (Jean Neal, pseudonym), *St. Louis Globe-Democrat*, July 10
"The Summer Man" (Jean Neal, pseudonym), *St. Louis Globe-Democrat*, July 31
"Picnics and Picnics" (Jean Neal, pseudonym), *St. Louis Globe-Democrat*, October 2

1899 "Mind Reader," *New England Magazine*, January
"A Sure Cure for the Blues" (Jean Neal, pseudonym), *St. Louis Globe-Democrat*, January 29
"Sarcophagus" (poem), *New England Magazine*, February
"The Way of Ruth," *New England Magazine*, March
"Anniversaries That Thrill" (Jean Neal, pseudonym), *St. Louis Globe-Democrat*, March 5
"The Man Who Played the Cymbals," *The Interior*, March 9
"May Day" (Jean Neal, pseudonym), *St. Louis Globe-Democrat*, April 30
"The Brotherless Girl" (Jean Neal, pseudonym), *St. Louis Globe-Democrat*, May 7
"The Engagement of One's Gentleman Friends" (Jean Neal, pseudonym), *St. Louis Globe-Democrat*, June 11
"Bachelor Girls in Scotland" (Jean Neal, pseudonym), *St. Louis Globe-Democrat*, July 30
"A Sisterly Office," *The Household*, August
"Bachelor Girls in the Land of Canals and Windmills" (Jean Neal, pseudonym), *St. Louis Globe-Democrat*, September 10

"Bachelor Girls in Kaiser William's Country" (Jean Neal, pseudonym), *St. Louis Globe-Democrat*, October 8
"Bachelor Girls in the Alps" (Jean Neal, pseudonym), *St. Louis Globe-Democrat*, October 22
"Bachelor Girls in Paris" (Jean Neal, pseudonym), *St. Louis Globe-Democrat*, November 5
"Bachelor Girls in London" (Jean Neal, pseudonym), *St. Louis Globe-Democrat*, November 19
"Bachelor Girls in Windsor Castle" (Jean Neal, pseudonym), *St. Louis Globe Democrat*, December 3

1900 "Faring Down the World" (poem), *New England Magazine*, January
"Ballad of the Little Page" (poem), *St. Nicholas*, February
"In a Library" (poem), *St. Nicholas*, March
"Crab Tree," *Munsey*, April
"Not at Home" (poem), *New England Magazine*, April
"Blessed Privilege" (poem), *New England Magazine*, July
"Notable Trees About Boston," *New England Magazine*, July
"The Barn Stormers," *The Ladies' World*, July
"The Seven Sleepers of Ephesus," *The Churchman*, July 28
"The Children's Crusade," *Radcliffe Magazine*, December

1901 "Family Reunion" (poem), *St. Nicholas*, September
"The Little Cassandra Turkey," *The Interior*, November 21
"Christmas Stories of the Saints," *Lippincott*, December

1902 "The Dissolving of a Partnership," *The Ladies' World*, September
"Neighbors," *Lippincott*, November
"Salaun, the Witless," *The Churchman*, November 1

1903 "Beauty of Antiquity," *New England Magazine*, May
"Old Ipswich Town," *New England Magazine*, June

1905 "The Mermaid Necklace," *The Churchman*, February 4, 11
"City Roofs" (poem), *Harper*, April
"The Yankee Balloon," *The Churchman*, July 1

1906 "The Faun Boys," *The Churchman*, January 20, 27

"Wanderlust" (poem), *Harper*, February
"Memory of Deacon Poole," *New England Magazine*, March
"The Dark Room," *The Churchman*, March 18
"The Educated Cat," *Good Housekeeping*, September
"Pages of J.T.T." (poem), *Poet Lore*, September

1907 "The Neighbor's Baby," *American Baby*, February
"This Sorry Scheme of Things" (poem), *Harper*, March
"Fireflies" (poem), *New England Magazine*, August
"Wonder Garden," *St. Nicholas*, September
"Thankful Cats," *The Churchman*, November 23

1908 "The Prize-Winner," *The Churchman*, January 11, 18, February 8, 15
"An Inconsistent Romance," *New England Magazine*, February
"To the Rescue," *The Congregationalist and the Christian World*, November 28
"The Cheerful Winters, A Christmas Story," *The Congregationalist and the Christian World*, December 19

1910 "Mr. Bear's Party," *Kindergarten Review*, October
"Bubbles" (poem), *Woman's Home Companion*, November

1911 "King's Pie" (poem), *St. Nicholas*, January
"Tree City" (poem), *St. Nicholas*, May
"Fisherman" (poem), *Good Housekeeping*, June
"Windows" (poem), *Outlook*, July
"Writing for Children," *The Writer*, September
"The Book and the Child," *Home Progress*, November
"Island Twins," *Woman's Home Companion*, (series begins in December)

1912 "Island Twins," *Woman's Home Companion*, (series ends in April)
"Transfigured" (poem), *Lippincott*, June
"Rose Perennial" (poem), *Literary Digest*, June
"The Adventures of Jim, and John and Jane," Denison Manufacturing Company, no month

1913 "Child's Poetry-books," *Home Progress*, January

	"The Dog Who Kept His Eyes Open," *Congregationalist*, February 6
	"Heritage" (poem), *Outlook*, March
	"Answers to Home Progress Questions Concerning Child Management," *Home Progress*, April
	"Bells That Brought Fairy Gold," *Woman's Home Companion*, June
	"Well-Wishing" (poem), *Woman's Home Companion*, July
	"An Inherited Tradition," *Sunday Magazine*, December 14
1914	"Mystery of Enchanted Oval," *Boston Post*, January 25
	"The Lucky Stone," *St. Nicholas*, January, February, March, April, May, June, July
	"Button, Button," *The Companion*, February 5
	"Magic Shoes," *Delineator*, June
	"A Star for Cadie," *Associated Sunday Magazine*, July 12
	"Luck-pluck" (poem), *St. Nicholas*, September
1915	"Where the Arrow Pointed," *Sunday School Advocate*, November 13, 20, 27, December 4, 11, 18, 26
1916	"The Goldfish Globe," *The Classmates*, January 15
	"Sparrow" (poem), *St. Nicholas*, July
	"The Sewing Circle," *The Churchman*, July 22
1917	"Concerning Halves" (poem), *Harper*, June
	"Secret" (poem), *St. Nicholas*, June
	"Cross-current" (poem), *Bellman*, December 15
1918	"Plume" (poem), *Bookman*, January
	"Maids and Mushrooms" (poem), *Bookman*, May
	"Knights" (poem), *Harper*, September
	"Fairy Ring" (poem), *Bellman*, September 8
1919	"Sylvia" (poem), *Ladies' Home Journal*, January
	"Every Day for a Hero" (poem), *St. Nicholas*, March
	"From the Canteen" (poem), *Delineator*, November
	"Mushrooms or Fairy Cats?" (poem), *Woman's Home Companion*, December

1920 "Pilgrims' Plymouth," *Delineator*, June
"Names" (poem), *Atlantic*, June
(same), *Literary Digest*, June 12
"Pilgrim Mothers" (poem), *Woman's Home Companion*, October
"Frightened Path" (poem), *Current Opinion*, November
"Scarecrow" (poem), *Current Opinion*, November
"Pirate Treasure" (poem), *Literary Digest*, November 6

1921 "Low Tide" (poem), *North American*, August
"The Tramper" (poem), *Christian Endeavor World*, November 1

1923 "Wild Grape" (poem), *Atlantic*, March
"Josephine Peabody, the Piper," *Bookman*, May
"Grandser" (poem), *Literary Digest*, July 21
"Robin the Thief" (poem), *St. Nicholas*, August

1925 "Dahlia" (poem), *Garden Monthly*, April
"Amy Lowell" (poem), *Literary Digest*, June 6

1926 "Ancient Humor" (poem), *Bookman*, February
"The Wonderful Arrow," *Children's Hour*, March
"Heroines" (poem), *St. Nicholas*, June
"Weather Vane" (poem), *Woman's Home Companion*, July
"Road Past the Dressmaker's House" (poem), *Woman's Home Companion*, October

1927 "To a Gloomy Poet" (poem), *Boston Transcript*, March 12
also appeared in *Contemporary Verse*, March

Stories—No Date

"Winged Boots," *The Young Churchman*
"The Yellow Day," *The Housewife*, (serial)
"The Square Fairies," *Sunday Magazine* of the *Sunday Post*

Books

1900 *The Book of Saints and Friendly Beasts* (Boston: Houghton Mifflin)
Notable Trees About Boston (Boston: Houghton Mifflin)

1901 *The Lonesomest Doll* (Boston: Houghton Mifflin)
(1928: Reprinted with the Arthur Rackham illustrations)

1902 *In the Days of Giants: A Book of Norse Tales* (Boston: Houghton Mifflin)
A Pocketful of Posies (Boston: Houghton Mifflin)

1903 *The Curious Book of Birds* (Boston: Houghton Mifflin)

1904 *The Flower Princess* (Boston: Houghton Mifflin)

1905 *The Star Jewels and Other Wonders* (Boston: Houghton Mifflin)

1906 *Brothers and Sisters* (Boston: Houghton Mifflin)

1907 *Friends and Cousins* (Boston: Houghton Mifflin)

1908 *Fresh Posies* (Boston: Houghton Mifflin)

1909 *John of the Woods* (Boston: Houghton Mifflin)
Tales of the Red Children (publisher not known; collab. with Jack Bell Mackintosh)

1910 *The Christmas Angel* (Boston: Houghton Mifflin)
The Boy Mozart (Boston: Parker, Baker and Taylor Publishing Co.)

1912 *Their City Christmas* (Boston: Houghton Mifflin)

1914 *The Lucky Stone* (New York: The Century Company)
Songs of Sixpence (Boston: Houghton Mifflin)

1915 *Kisington Town* (Boston: Houghton Mifflin)

1917 *Surprise House* (Boston: Houghton Mifflin)

1918 *Rock of Liberty* ["Peace with a Sword"] Music by Rossetter G. Cole. (Boston: Arthur P. Schmidt Co.)

1920 *Heart of New England* (Boston: Houghton Mifflin)

1921 *Round Robin* (E. P. Dutton & Company)

1922 *The Lights of Beacon Hill* (Boston: Houghton Mifflin)

1924 *The Boyhood of Edward MacDowell* (New York: Frederick A Stokes)

1925 *The Christmas Tree* (Boston: Houghton Mifflin)

1926 *The Silver Stair* (Boston: Houghton Mifflin)
Under the Rowan Tree (Boston: Houghton Mifflin)

1927 *The Lantern and Other Plays* (Boston: Houghton Mifflin; reprinted by Core Collection Books in 1978)

1960 *The Little Friend* (excerpted from *The Flower Princess;* Boston: Houghton Mifflin)

Although many sources were used for this list of works, special thanks and appreciation are due the staff of the Schlesinger Library of Radcliffe College at Harvard University.

Chapter 1

The Play Box

T the sound of footsteps along the hall Miss Terry looked up from the letter which she was reading for the sixth time. "Of course I would not see him," she said, pursing her lips into a hard line. "Certainly not!"

A bump on the library door, as from an opposing knee, did duty for a knock.

"Bring the box in here, Norah," said Miss Terry, holding open the door for her servant, who was gasping under the weight of a packing case. "Set it down on the rug by the fireplace. I am going to look it over and burn up the rubbish this evening."

She glanced once more at the letter in her hand, then with a sniff tossed it upon the fire.

"Yes'm," said Norah, as she set down the box with a thump. She stooped once more to pick up something which had fallen out when the cover was jarred open. It was a pink papier-mâché angel, such as are often hung from the top of Christmas trees as a crowning symbol. Norah stood holding it between thumb and finger, staring amazedly. Who would think to find such a bit of frivolity in the house of Miss Terry!

Her mistress looked up from the fire, where the bit of writing was writhing painfully, and caught the expression on Norah's face.

"What have you there?" she asked, frowning, as she took the object into her own hands. "The Christmas angel!" she exclaimed under her breath. "I had quite forgotten it." Then as if it burned her fingers she thrust the little figure back into the box and turned to Norah brusquely. "There, that's all. You can go now, Norah," she said.

"Yes'm," answered the maid. She hesitated. "If you please 'm, it's Christmas Eve."

"Well, I believe so," snapped Miss Terry, who seemed to be in a particularly bad humor this evening. "What do you want?"

Norah flushed; but she was hardened to her mistress's manner. "Only to ask if I may go out for a little while to see the decorations and hear the singing."

"Decorations? Singing? Fiddlesticks!" retorted Miss Terry, poker in hand. "What decorations? What singing?"

"Why, all the windows along the street are full of candles," answered Norah, "rows of candles in every house, to light the Christ Child on his way when he comes through the city tonight."

"Fiddlesticks!" again snarled her mistress.

"And choirboys are going about the streets, they say, singing carols in front of the lighted houses," continued Norah enthusiastically. "It must sound so pretty!"

"They had much better be at home in bed. I believe people are losing their minds!"

"Please 'm, may I go?" asked Norah again.

Norah had no puritanical[1] traditions to her account. Moreover she was young and warm and enthusiastic. Sometimes the spell of Miss Terry's somber house threatened her to the point of desperation. It was so this Christmas Eve; but she made her request with apparent calmness.

"Yes, go along," answered her mistress ungraciously.

"Thank you, 'm," said the servant demurely, but with a brightening of her blue eyes. And presently the area door banged behind her quick-retreating footsteps.

"H'm! Didn't take her long to get ready!" muttered Miss Terry, giving the fire a vicious poke. She was alone in the house, on Christmas Eve, and not a man, woman, or child in the world cared. Well, it was what she wanted. It was of her own doing. If she had wished —

She sat back in her chair, with thin, long hands lying along the arms of it, gazing into the fire. A bit of paper there was crumbling into ashes. Alone on Christmas Eve! Even Norah had some relation with the world outside. Was there not a stalwart officer waiting for her on the nearest corner? Even Norah could feel a simple childish pleasure in candles and carols and merriment, and the old, old superstition.

---

1 The Puritans banned all Christmas celebrations during the Commonwealth Period in England.

"Stuff and nonsense!" mused Miss Terry scornfully. "What is our Christmas, anyway? A time for shopkeepers to sell and for foolish folks to kill themselves in buying. Christmas spirit? No! It is all humbug—all selfishness, and worry; an unwholesome season of unnatural activities. I am glad I am out of it. I am glad no one expects anything of me—nor I of anyone. I am quite independent; blessedly independent of the whole foolish business. It is a good time to begin clearing up for the new year. I'm glad I thought of it. I've long threatened to get rid of the stuff that has been accumulating in that corner of the attic. Now I will begin."

She tugged the packing case an inch nearer the fire. It was like Miss Terry to insist upon that nearer inch. Then she raised the cover. It was a box full of children's battered toys, old-fashioned and quaint; the toys in vogue thirty—forty—fifty years earlier, when Miss Terry was a child. She gave a reminiscent sniff as she threw up the cover and saw on the under side of it a big label of pasteboard unevenly lettered.

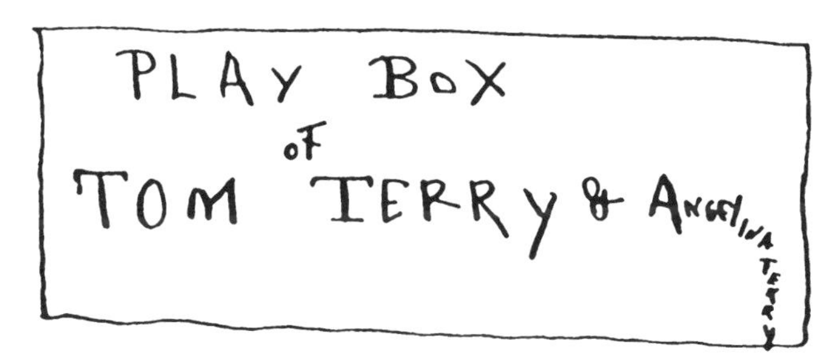

"Humph!" she snorted. There was a great deal in that "humph." It meant: Yes, Tom's name had plenty of room, while poor little Angelina had to squeeze in as well as she could. How like Tom! This accounted for everything, even to his not being in his sister's house this very night. How unreasonable he had been!

Miss Terry shrugged impatiently. Why think of Tom tonight? Years ago he had deliberately cut himself adrift from her interests. No need to think of him now. It was too late to appease her. But here were all these toys to be got rid of. The fire was hungry for them. Why not begin?

Miss Terry stooped to poke over the contents of the box with lean, long fingers. In one corner thrust up a doll's arm; in another, an animal's tail pointed heavenward. She caught glimpses of glitter and tinsel, wheels and fragments of unidentifiable toys.

"What rubbish!" she said. "Yes, I'll burn them all. They are good for nothing else. I suppose some folks would try to give them away, and bore a lot of people to death. They seem to think they are saving something, that way. Nonsense! I know better. It is all foolishness, this craze for giving. Most things are better destroyed as soon as you are done with them. Why, nobody wants such truck as this. Now, could any child ever have cared for so silly a thing?" She pulled out a faded jumping jack, and regarded it scornfully. "Idiotic! Such toys are demoralizing for children—weakens their minds. It is a shame to think how everyone seems bound to spoil children, especially at Christmastime. Well, no one can say that I have added to the shameful waste."

Miss Terry tossed the poor jumping jack on the fire, and eyed his last contortions with grim satisfaction.

But as she watched, a quaint idea came to her. She was famous for eccentric ideas.

"I will try an experiment," she said. "I will prove once and for all my point about the 'Christmas spirit.' I will drop some of these old toys out on the sidewalk and see what happens. It may be interesting."

Chapter 2

JACK-IN-THE-BOX

ISS Terry rose and crossed two rooms to the front window, looking out upon the street. A flare of light almost blinded her eyes. Every window opposite her along the block, as far as she could see, was illuminated with a row of lighted candles across the sash. The soft, unusual glow threw into relief the pretty curtains and wreaths of green, and gave glimpses of cozy interiors and flitting happy figures.

"What a waste of candles!" scolded Miss Terry. "Folks are growing terribly extravagant."

The street was white with snow which had fallen a few hours earlier, piled in drifts along the curb of the little-traveled terrace. But the sidewalks were neatly shoveled and swept clean, as became the eminently respectable part of the city where Miss Terry lived. A long flight of steps, with iron railing at the side, led down from the front door, upon which a silver plate had for generations in decorous flourishes announced the name of Terry.

Miss Terry returned to the play box and drew out between thumb and finger the topmost toy. It happened to be a wooden box, with a wire hasp for fastening the cover. Half unconsciously she pressed the spring, and a hideous jack-in-the-box sprang out to confront her with a squeak, a leering smile, and a red nose. Miss Terry eyed him with disfavor.

"I always did hate that thing," she said. "Tom was continually frightening me with it, I remember." As if to be rid of unwelcome memories she shut her mouth tight, even as she shut Jack back into his box, snapping the spring into place. *This will do to begin with,* she thought. She crossed to the window, which she opened quickly, and tossed out the box, so that it fell squarely in the middle of the sidewalk. Then closing the window and turning down the lights in the room behind her, Miss Terry hid in the folds of the curtains and watched to see what would happen to Jack.

The street was quiet. Few persons passed on either side. At last she spied two little ragamuffins approaching. They seemed to be Jewish lads of the newsboy class, and they eyed the display of candles appraisingly. The smaller boy first caught sight of the box in the middle of the sidewalk.

"Hello! Wot's dis?" he grunted, making a dash upon it.

"Gee! Wot's up?" responded the other, who was instantly at his elbow. "Gwan! Lemme look at it."

The smaller boy drew away and pressed the spring of the box eagerly. *Ping!* Out popped the Jack into his astonished face; whereupon he set up a guffaw.

"Give it here!" commanded the bigger boy.

"Naw! You let it alone! It's mine!" asserted the other, edging away along the curbstone. "I saw it first. You can't have it."

"Give it here. I saw it first myself. Hand it over, or I'll smash you!"

The bigger boy advanced threateningly.

"I won't!" the other whimpered, clasping the box tightly under his jacket.

He started to run, but the bigger fellow was too quick for him. He pounced across the sidewalk, and soon the twain were struggling in the snowdrift, pummeling one another with might and main.

"I told you so!" commented Miss Terry from behind the curtain. "Here's the first show of the beautiful Christmas spirit that is supposed to be abroad. Look at the little beasts fighting over something that neither of them really wants!"

Just then Miss Terry spied a blue-coated figure leisurely approaching. At the same moment an instinct seemed to warn the struggling urchins.

"Cop!" said a muffled voice from the pile of arms and legs, and in an instant two black shadows were flitting down the street; but not before the bigger boy had wrenched the box from the pocket of the little chap.

"So that is the end of experiment number one," quoth Miss Terry, smiling grimly. "It happened just about as I expected. They will be fighting again as soon as they are out of sight. They are Jews; but that doesn't make any difference about the Christmas spirit. Now let's see what becomes of the next experiment."

Chapter 3

THE FLANTON DOG

HE returned to the play box by the fire, and rummaged for a few minutes among the tangled toys. Then with something like a chuckle she drew out a soft, pale creature with four wobbly legs.

"The Flanton dog!" she said. "Well, I vow! I had forgotten all about him. It was Tom who coined the name for him because he was made of Canton flannel."

She stood the thing up on the table as well as his weak legs would allow, and inspected him critically. He certainly was a forlorn specimen. One of the black beads which had served him for eyes was gone. His ears, which had originally stood up saucily on his head, now drooped in limp dejection. One of them was a mere shapeless rag hanging by a thread. He was dirty and discolored, and his tail was gone. But still he smiled with his red-thread mouth and seemed trying to make the best of things.

"What a nightmare!" said Miss Terry contemptuously. "I know there isn't a child in the city who wants such a wretched-looking thing. Why, even the animal rescue folks would give the boys a 'free shot' at that. This isn't going to bring out any Christmas spirit," she sneered. "I will try it and see."

Once more she lifted the window and tossed the dog to the sidewalk. He rolled upon his back and lay pathetically with crooked legs yearning upward, still smiling. Hardly had Miss Terry time to conceal herself behind the curtain when she saw a figure approaching, airily waving a stick.

"No ragamuffin this time," she said. "Hello! It is that good-for-nothing young Cooper fellow from the next block. They say he is a millionaire. Well, he isn't even going to see the Flanton dog."

The young man came swinging along, debonairly; he was whistling under his breath. He was a dapper figure in a long coat and a silk hat, under which the candles lighted a rather silly face. When he reached the spot in the sidewalk where the Flanton dog lay, he paused a moment looking down. Then he poked the object with his stick. On the other side of the street a mother and her little boy were passing at the time. The child's eyes caught sight of the dog on the sidewalk, and he hung back, watching to see what the young man would do to it. But his mother drew him after her. Just then an automobile came panting through the snow. With a quick movement Cooper picked up the dog on the end of his stick and tossed it into the street, under the wheels of the machine. The child across the street uttered a howl of anguish at the sight. Miss Terry herself was surprised to feel a pang shoot through her as the car passed over the queer old toy. She retreated from the window quickly.

"Well, that's the end of Flanton," she said with half a sigh. "I knew that fellow was a brute. I might have expected something like that. But it looked so . . . so . . ." She hesitated for a word, and did not finish her sentence, but bit her lip and sniffed cynically.

Chapter 4

THE NOAH'S ARK

OW, what comes next?" Miss Terry rummaged in the box until her fingers met something odd-shaped, long, and smooth-sided. With some difficulty she drew out the object, for it was of good size.

"H'm! The old Noah's ark," she said. "I wonder if all the animals are in there."

She lifted the cover, and turned out into her lap the long-imprisoned animals and their round-bodied chief. Mrs. Noah and her sons had long since disappeared. But the ark-builder, hatless and one-armed, still presided over a menagerie of sorry beasts. Scarcely one could boast of being a quadruped. To few of them the years had spared a tail. From their close resemblance in their misery, it was not hard to believe in the kinship of all animal life. She took them up and examined them curiously one by one. Finally she selected a shapeless slate-colored block from the mass. "This was the elephant," she mused. "I remember when Tom stepped on him and smashed his trunk. 'I guess I'm going to be an expressman when I grow up,' he said, looking sorry. Tom was always full of his jokes. Now I'll try this and see what happens to the ark on its last voyage."

Just then there was a noise outside. An automobile honked past, and Miss Terry shuddered, recalling the pathetic end of the Flanton dog, which had given her quite a turn.

"I hate those horrid machines!" she exclaimed. "They seem like juggernaut. I'd like to forbid their going through this street."

She crowded the elephant with Noah and the rest of his charge back into the ark and closed the lid. "I can't throw this out of the window," she reflected. "They would spill. I must take it out on the sidewalk. Land! The fire's going out! That girl doesn't know how to build fires so they will keep."

She laid the Noah's ark on the table, and going to the closet tugged out several big logs, which she arranged geometrically. About laying fires, as about most other things, Miss Terry had her own positive theories. Taking the bellows in hand she blew furiously, and was presently rewarded with a brisk blaze. She smiled with satisfaction, and trotted upstairs to find her red knit shawl. With this about her shoulders she was prepared to brave the December cold. Down the steps she went, and deposited the ark discreetly at their foot; then returned to take up her position behind the curtains.

There were a good many people passing, but they seemed too preoccupied to glance down at the sidewalk. They were nearly all hurrying in one direction. Some were running in the middle of the street.

"They are in a great hurry," sniffed Miss Terry disdainfully. "One would think they had something really important to do. I suppose they are going to hear the singing. Fiddlesticks!"

A man hastened by under the window; a woman; two children, a boy and a girl, running and gesticulating eagerly. None of them noticed the Noah's ark lying at the foot of the steps.

Miss Terry began to grow impatient. "Are they all blind?" she fretted. "What is the matter with them? I wish somebody would find the thing. I am tired of seeing it lying there."

She tapped the floor impatiently with her slipper. Just then a woman approached. She was dressed in the most uncompromising of mourning, and she walked slowly, with bent head, never glancing at the lighted windows on either side.

"She will see it," commented Miss Terry. And sure enough, she did. She stopped at the doorway, drew her skirts aside, and bent over to look at the strange-shaped box at her feet. Finally she lifted it. But immediately she shivered and acted so strangely that Miss Terry thought she was about to break the toy in pieces on the steps or throw it into the street. Evidently she detested the sight of it.

Just then up came a second woman with two small boys hanging at her skirts. They were ragged and sick-looking. There was something about the expression of even the tiny knot of hair at the back of the woman's head which told of anxious poverty. With envious curiosity she hurried up to see what a luckier mortal had found, crowding to look over her shoulder. The woman in black drew haughtily away and clutched the Noah's ark with a gesture of proprietorship.

Go away! This is my affair. Miss Terry read her expression and sniffed.

"There is the Christmas spirit coming out again," she said to herself. "Look at her face!"

The black-gowned woman prepared to move on with the toy under the arm. But the second woman caught hold of her skirt and began to speak earnestly. She pointed to the Noah's ark, then to her two children. Her eyes were beseeching. The little boys crowded forward eagerly. But some wicked spirit seemed to have seized the finder of the ark. Angrily she shook off the hand of the other woman, and clutching the box yet more firmly under her arm, she hurried away. Once, twice, she turned and shook her head at the ragged woman who followed her. Then, with a savage gesture at the two children, she disappeared beyond Miss Terry's straining eyes. The poor woman and her boys followed forlornly at a distance.

"They really wanted it, that old Noah's ark!" exclaimed Miss Terry in amazement. "I can scarcely believe it. But why did that other creature keep the thing? I see! Only because she found they cared for it. Well, that is a happy spirit for Christmastime, I should say! Humph! I did not expect to find anything quite so mean as *that!*"

Chapter 5

MIRANDA

ISS Terry returned to the fireside, fumbled in the box, and drew out a doll. She was an ugly, old-fashioned doll, with bruised waxen face of no particular color. Her mop of flaxen hair was straggling and uneven, much the worse for the attention given by generations of moths. She wore a faded green silk dress in the style of Lincoln's day, and a primitive bonnet, evidently made by childish hands. She was a strange, dead-looking figure, with pale eyelids closed, as Miss Terry dragged her from the box. But when she was set upright the lids snapped open and a pair of bright blue eyes looked straight into those of Miss Terry. It was so sudden that the lady nearly gasped.

"Miranda!" she exclaimed. "It is old Miranda! I have not thought of her for years." She held the doll at arm's length, gazing fixedly at her for some minutes.

"I cannot burn her," she muttered at last. "It would seem almost like murder. I don't like to throw her away, but I have vowed to get rid of these things tonight. And I'll do it, anyway. Yes, I'll make an experiment of her. I wonder what sort of trouble she will cause.

Not even Miss Terry could think of seeing old Miranda lying exposed to the winter night. She found a piece of paper, rolled up the doll in a neat package, and tied it with red string. It was, to look upon, entirely a tempting package. Once more she stole down the steps and hesitated where to leave Miranda. Not on the sidewalk—for some reason that seemed impossible. But near the foot of the flight of steps leading to the front door she deposited the doll. The white package shone out plainly in the illuminated street. There was no doubt that it would be readily seen.

With a quite unexplainable interest Miss Terry watched to see what would happen to Miranda. She waited for some time. The street seemed deserted. Miss Terry caught the faint sound of singing. The choristers were passing through a neighboring street, and doubtless all wayfarers within hearing of their voices were following in their wake.

She was thoroughly interested in her grim joke, but she was becoming impatient. Were there to be no more people passing by? Must the doll stay there unclaimed until morning? Presently she became aware of a child's figure drawing near. It was a little girl of about ten, very shabbily dressed, with tangled yellow curls hanging over her shoulders. There was something familiar about her appearance, but Miss Terry could not say what it was. She came hurrying along the sidewalk with a preoccupied air, and seemed about to pass the steps without seeing the package lying there. But just as she was opposite the window, her eye caught the gleam of the white paper. She paused. She looked at it eagerly; it was such a tempting package, both as to its size and shape! She went closer and bent down to examine it. She took it into her bare little hands and seemed to squeeze it gently. There is no mistaking the contours of a doll, however well it may be enveloped in paper wrappings. The child's eyes grew more and more eager. She glanced behind her furtively; she looked up and down the street. Then with a sudden intuition she looked straight ahead, up the flight of stairs.

Miss Terry read her mind accurately. She was thinking that probably the doll belonged in that house; someone must have dropped the package while going out or in. Would she ring the bell and return it? Miss Terry had not thought of that possibility. But she shook her head and her lip curled. "Return it? Of course not! Ragged children do not usually return promising packages which they have found—even on Christmas Eve. Look now!"

Once more the child glanced stealthily behind her, up and down the street. Once more she looked up at the dark house before her, the only black spot in a wreath of brilliancy. She did not see the face peering at her through the curtains, a face which scanned her own half wistfully. What was to become of Miranda? The little girl thrust the package under her ragged coat and ran away down the street as fast as her legs could take her.

"A thief!" cried Miss Terry. "That is the climax. I have detected a child taking what she knew did not belong to her, on Christmas Eve! Where are all their Sunday school lessons and their social improvement classes? I knew it! This Christmas spirit that one hears so much about is nothing

SHE LOOKED UP AND DOWN THE STREET

but an empty sham. I have proved it to my satisfaction tonight. I will burn the rest of these toys, every one of them, and then go to bed. It is too disgusting! She was a nice-looking child, too. Poor old Miranda!"

With something like a sigh Miss Terry strode back to the fire, where the play box stood gaping. She had made but a small inroad upon its heaped-up treasures. She threw herself listlessly into the chair and began to plow through the things in her box. Broken games and animals, dolls' dresses painfully tailored by unskilled fingers, disjointed members—sorry relics of past pleasures—one by one Miss Terry seized them between disdainful thumb and finger and tossed them into the fire. Her face showed not a qualm at parting with these childhood treasures; only the stern sense of a good housekeeper's duty fulfilled. With queer contortions the bits writhed on the coals, and finally flared into dissolution, vanishing up chimney in a shower of sparks to the heaven of spent toys.

Chapter 6

The Christmas Angel

LMOST at the bottom of the box Miss Terry's fingers closed about a small object. Once more she drew out the papier-mâché angel which had so excited the wonder of Norah when once before that evening it had come to light.

Miss Terry held it up and looked at it with the same expression on her face, half tender, half contemptuous. "The Christmas angel!" she murmured involuntarily, as she had done before. And again there flashed through her mind a vivid picture.

It was the day before Christmas, fifty years earlier. She and her brother Tom were trimming the Christmas tree in this very library. She saw Tom, in a white piqué suit with short socks that were always slipping down his fat legs. She saw herself in a white dress and blue ribbons, pouting in a corner. They had been quarreling about the Christmas tree, disputing as to which of them should light the first candle[2] when the time arrived. Then their mother came to them smiling, a sweet-faced lady who seemed not to notice the red faces and the tears. She put something into Tom's hand saying, "This is the Christmas angel of peace and goodwill. Hang it on the tree, children, so that it may shed a blessing on all who come here to give and to receive."

How lovely and pink it looked in Tom's hand! Little Angelina had thought it the most beautiful thing she had ever seen—and holy, too, as if it had some blessed charm. *Fiddlesticks! What queer fancies children have!* Miss Terry remembered how a strange thrill had crept through Angelina as she gazed at it. Then she and Tom looked at each other and were

2 In pre-electric light times, candles were placed on the branches, for Christmas illumination and atmosphere—obviously, the fire danger was high.

ashamed of their quarrel. Suddenly Tom held out the angel to his sister. "You hang it on the tree, Angelina," he said magnanimously. "I know you want to."

But she—little fool!—she too had a fit of generosity.

"No, you hang it, Tom. You're taller," she said.

"I'll hang it at the very top of the tree!" he replied, nothing loath. Eagerly he mounted the stepladder, while Angelina watched him enviously, thinking how clumsy he was, and how much better she could do it.

How funny and fat Tom had looked on top of the ladder, reaching as high as he dared! The ladder began to wobble, and he balanced precariously, while Angelina clutched at his fat ankles with a scream of fright. But Tom said:

"Ow! Angelina, let go my ankles! You hurt! Now don't scream. I shan't fall. Don't you know that this is the Christmas angel, and he will never let me get hurt on Christmas Eve?"

Swaying wildly on one toe Tom had clutched at the air, at the tree itself—anywhere for support. Yet, almost as if by a miracle, he did not fall. And the Christmas angel was looking down from the very top of the tree.

Miss Terry laid the little pink figure in her lap and mused. "Mother was wise!" she sighed. "She knew how to settle our quarrels in those days. Perhaps if she had still been here things would have gone differently. Tom might not have left me for good. *For good.*" She emphasized the words with a nod as if arguing against something.

Again she took up the Christmas angel and looked earnestly at it. Could it be that tears were glistening in her eyes? Certainly not! With a sudden sniff and jerk of the shoulders she leaned forward, holding the angel towards the fire. This should follow the other useless toys. But something seemed to stay her hand. She drew back, hesitated, then rose to her feet.

"I can't burn it," she said. "It's no use, I can't burn it. But I don't want to see the thing around. I will put this out on the sidewalk, too. Possibly this may be different and do some good to somebody."

She wrapped the shawl about her shoulders and once more ran down the steps. She left the angel face upward in the middle of the sidewalk, and retreated quickly to the house. As she opened the door to enter, she caught the distant chorus of fresh young voices singing in a neighboring square:

> Angels from the realms of glory,
> Wing your flight o'er all the earth

When she took her place behind the curtain she was trembling a little, she could not guess why. But now she watched with renewed eagerness. What was to be the fate of the Christmas angel? Would he fall into the right hands and be hung upon some Christmas tree ere morning? Would he . . .

Miss Terry held her breath. A man was staggering along the street toward her. He whistled noisily a vulgar song, as he reeled from curb to railing, threatening to fall at every step. A drunken man on Christmas Eve! Miss Terry felt a great loathing for him. He was at the foot of the steps now. He was close upon the angel. Would he see it, or would he tread upon it in his disgusting blindness?

Yes—no! He saw the little pink image lying on the bricks, and with a lurch forward bent to examine it. Miss Terry flattened her nose against the pane eagerly. She expected to see him fall upon the angel bodily. But no; he righted himself with a whoop of drunken mirth.

"Angel!" she heard him croak with maudlin accent. "Pink angel, begorra![3] What doin' 'ere, eh? Whoop! Go back to sky, angel!" and lifting a brutal foot he kicked the image into the street. Then with a shriek of laughter he staggered away out of sight.

Miss Terry found herself trembling with indignation. The idea! He had kicked the Christmas angel—the very angel that Tom had hung on their tree! It was sacrilege, or at least—Fiddlesticks! Miss Terry's mind was growing confused. She had a sudden impulse to rescue the toy from being trampled into filthiness. The fire was better than that.

She hurried down the steps into the street, forgetting her shawl. She sought in the snow and snatched the pink morsel to safety. Straight to the fire she carried it, and once more held it out to the flames. But again she found it impossible to burn the thing. Once, twice, she tried. But each time something seemed to snatch back her wrist. At last she shrugged impatiently and laid the angel on the mantelpiece beside the square, old marble clock, which marked the hour of half past eight.

"Well, I won't burn it tonight," she reflected. "Somehow, I can't do it just now. I don't see what has got into me! But tomorrow I will. Yes, tomorrow I will."

She sat down in the armchair and fumbled in the old play box for the remaining scraps. There were but a few meaningless bits of ribbon and

3 Irish expression meaning "It's a fine day!"

gauze, with the end of a Christmas candle, the survivor of some past festival, burned on some tree in the past. All these but the last she tossed into the fire, where they made a final protesting blaze. The candle end fell to the floor unnoticed.

"There! That is the last of the stuff," she exclaimed with grim satisfaction, shaking the dust from her black silk skirt. "It is all gone now, thank Heaven, and I can go to bed in peace. No, I forgot Norah. I suppose I must sit up and wait for her. Bother the girl! She ought to be in by now. What can she find to amuse her all this time? Christmas Eve! Fiddlesticks! But I have got rid of a lot of rubbish tonight, and that is worth something."

She sank back in her chair and clasped her hands over her breast with a sigh. She felt strangely weary. Her eyes sought the clock once more, and doing so rested upon the Christmas angel lying beside it. She frowned and closed her eyes to shut out the sight with its haunting memories and suggestions.

Chapter 7

BEFORE THE FIRE

UDDENLY there was a volume of sound outside, and a great brightness filled the room. Miss Terry opened her eyes. The fire was burning red; but a yellow light, as from thousands of candles, shone in at the window, and there was the sound of singing—the sweetest singing that Miss Terry had ever heard.

An angel of the Lord came down,
And glory shone around

The words seemed chanted by the voices of young angels. Miss Terry passed her hands over her eyes and glanced at the clock. But what the hour was she never noticed, for her gaze was filled with something else. Beside the clock, in the spot where she had laid it a few minutes before, was the Christmas angel. But now, instead of lying helplessly on its back, it was standing on rosy feet, with arms outstretched toward her. Over its head fluttered gauzy wings. From under the yellow hair which rippled over the shoulders two blue eyes beamed kindly upon her, and the mouth widened into the sweetest smile.

"Peace on earth to men of goodwill!" cried the angel, and the tone of his speech was music, yet quite natural and thrilling.

Miss Terry stared hard at the angel and rubbed her eyes, saying to herself, "Fiddlesticks! I am dreaming!"

But she could not rub away the vision. When she opened her eyes the angel still stood tiptoe on the mantel-shelf, smiling at her and shaking his golden head.

"Angelina!" said the angel softly; and Miss Terry trembled to hear her name thus spoken for the first time in years. "Angelina, you do not want to believe your own eyes, do you? But I am real; more real than the things you see every day. You must believe in me. I am the Christmas angel."

"I know it." Miss Terry's voice was hoarse and unmanageable, as of one in a nightmare. "I remember."

"You remember!" repeated the angel. "Yes; you remember the day when you and Tom hung me on the Christmas tree. You were a sweet little girl then, with blue eyes and yellow curls. You believed the Christmas story and loved Santa Claus. Then you were simple and affectionate and generous and happy."

"Fiddlesticks!" Miss Terry tried to say. But the word would not come.

"Now you have lost the old belief and the old love," went on the angel. "Now you have studied books and read wise men's sayings. You understand the higher criticism, and the higher charity, and the higher egoism. You don't believe in mere giving. You don't believe in the Christmas spirit—you know better. But are you happy, dear Angelina?"

Again Miss Terry thrilled to the sound of her name so sweetly spoken; but she answered nothing. The angel replied for her.

"No, you are not happy because you have cut yourself off from the things that bring folk together in peace and goodwill at this holy time. Where are your friends? Where is your brother tonight? You are still hard and unforgiving to Tom. You refused to see him today, though he wrote so boyishly, so humbly and affectionately. You have not tried to make any soul happy. You don't believe in *me*, the Christmas spirit."

There is such a word as *Fiddlesticks*, whatever it may mean. But Miss Terry's mind and tongue were unable to form it.

"The Christmas spirit!" continued the angel. "What is life worth if one cannot believe in the Christmas spirit?"

With a powerful effort Miss Terry shook off her nightmare sufficiently to say, "The Christmas spirit is no real thing. I have proved it tonight. It is not real. It is a humbug!"

"Not real? A humbug?" repeated the angel softly. "And you have proved it, Angelina, this very night?"

Miss Terry nodded.

"I know what you have done," said the angel. "I know very well. How keen you were! How clever! You made a test of chance, to prove your point."

Again Miss Terry nodded with complacency.

"What knowledge of the world! What grasp of human nature!" commented the angel, smiling. "It is like you mere mortals to say, 'I will make my test in my own way. If certain things happen, I shall foresee what the result must be. If certain other things happen, I shall know that I am right.' Events fall out as you expect, and you smile with satisfaction, feeling your wisdom justified. It ought to make you happy. But does it?"

Miss Terry regarded the angel doubtfully.

"Look now!" he went on, holding up a rosy finger. "You are so near-sighted! You are so unimaginative! You do not dream beyond the thing you see. You judge the tale finished while the best has yet to be told. And you stake your faith, your hope, your charity upon this blind human judgment—which is mere chance!"

Miss Terry opened her lips to say, "I saw—" but the angel interrupted her.

"You saw but the beginning," he said. "You saw but the first page of each history. Shall I turn over the leaves and let you read what really happened? Shall I help you to see the whole truth instead of a part? On this night holy truth, which is of Heaven, comes for all men to see and to believe. Look!"

Chapter 8

JACK AGAIN

HE Christmas angel gently waved his hand to and fro. Gradually, as Miss Terry sat back in her chair, the library grew dark; or rather, things faded into an indistinguishable blur. Then it seemed as if she were sitting at a theater gazing at a great stage. But at this theater there was nothing about her, nothing between her and the place where things were happening.

First she saw two little ragamuffins quarreling over something in the snow. She recognized them. They were the two Jewish boys who had picked up the jack-in-the-box. An officer appeared, and they ran away, the bigger boy having possession of the toy; the smaller one with fists in his eyes, bawling with disappointment.

Miss Terry's lips curled with the cynical disgust which she had felt when first witnessing this scene. But a sweet voice—and she knew it was the angel's—whispered in her ear, "Wait and see!"

She watched the two boys run through the streets until they came to a dark corner. There the little fellow caught up with the other, and once more the struggle began. It was a hard and bloody fight. But this time the victory was with the smaller lad, who used his fists and feet like an enraged animal, until the other howled for mercy and handed over the disputed toy.

"Whatcher want it fer, Sam?" he blubbered as he saw it go into the little fellow's pocket.

"Mind yer own business! I just want it," answered Sam surlily.

"Betcher I know," taunted the bigger boy.

"Betcher yer don't."

"Do!"

"Don't!"

Another fight seemed imminent. But wisdom prevailed with Sammy. He would not challenge fate a third time. "Come on, then, and see," he grunted.

And Ike followed. Off the two trudged, through the brilliantly lighted streets, until they came to a part of the city where the ways were narrower and dark.

"Huh! Knowed you was comin' here," commented Ike as they turned into a grim, dirty alley.

Little Sam growled, "Didn't!" apparently as a matter of habit.

"Did!" reasserted Ike. "Just where I was comin' myself."

Sam turned to him with a grin.

"Was yer now? By . . . ! Ain't that funny? I thought of it right off."

"Sure. Same here!"

They both burst into a guffaw and executed an impromptu double-shuffle of delight. They were at the door of a tenement house with steep stairs leading into darkness. Up three flights pounded the two pairs of heavy boots, till they reached a half-open door, whence issued the clatter of a sewing machine and the voices of children. Sam stood on the threshold grinning debonairly, with hands thrust into his pockets. Ike peered over his shoulder, also grinning.

It was a meager room into which they gazed, a room the chief furniture of which seemed to be babies. Two little ones sprawled on the floor. A third tiny tot lay in a broken-down carriage beside the door. A pale, ill-looking woman was running the machine. On the cot bed was crumpled a fragile little fellow of about five, and a small pair of crutches lay across the foot of the bed.

When the two boys appeared in the doorway, the woman stopped her machine and the children set up a howl of pleasure. "Sammy! Ikey!" cried the woman, smiling a wan welcome, as the babies crept and toddled toward the newcomers. "Where ye come from?"

"Been to see the shops and the lights in the swell houses," answered Sammy with a grimace. "Gee! Ain't they wastin' candles to beat the band!"

"Enough to last a family a whole year," muttered Ike with disgust.

The woman sighed. "Maybe they ain't wasted exactly," she said. "How I'd like to see 'em! But I got to finish this job. I told the chil'ren they mustn't expect anything this Christmas. But they are too little to know the difference anyway; all but Joe. I wish I had something for Joe."

"I got something for Joe," said Sammy unexpectedly.

The face of the pale little cripple lighted.

"What is it?" he asked eagerly. "Oh, what is it? A real Christmas present for me?"

"Naw! It ain't a Christmas present," said Sam.

"We don't care anything about Christmas," volunteered Ikey with a grin.

Sam looked at him with a frown of rebuke.

"It's just a *present,*" he said. And it didn't cost a cent. I didn't buy it. I—we found it!"

"Found it in the street?" Joe's eyes shone.

"Yah!" the boys nodded.

"Oh, it *is* a Christmas present!" cried Joe. "Santa Claus must have dropped it there for me, because he knew we hadn't any chimney in this house, and he sent you kind, kind boys to bring it to me."

The two urchins looked sideways at each other, but said nothing. Presently Sam drew out the box from his pocket and tried to thrust it into Ike's hand. "You give it to 'em," he said. "You're the biggest."

"Naw! You give it. You found it," protested Ike.

"Ah, g'wan!"

"Big fool!"

There was a tussle, and it almost seemed as if the past unpleasantness was to be repeated from an opposite cause. But Joe's voice settled the dispute.

"Oh, Sammy, please!" he cried. "I can't wait another minute. Do please give it to me now!"

At these words Sam stepped forward without further argument and laid the box on the bed in front of the little cripple. The babies crowded about. The mother left her machine and stood smiling faintly at the foot of the bed.

Joe pressed the spring. *Ping!* Out sprang the jack-in-the-box, with the same red nose, the same leer, the same roguish eyes which had surprised the children of fifty years ago.

Jack was always sure of his audience. My! How they screamed and begged Joe to "do it again." And as for Joe, he lay back on his pillow and laughed and laughed as though he would never stop. It was the first Jack any of them had ever seen.

Tears stood in the mother's eyes. "Well," she said, "it's as good as a play to see him. Joe hasn't laughed like that for months. You boys have done him lots of good. I wouldn't wonder if it helped him get well! If you was

PING! OUT SPRANG THE JACK-IN-THE-BOX

Christians I'd say you showed the real Christmas spirit. But—perhaps ye do, all the same! I dunno!"

Sam and Ike were so busy playing with the children that they did not hear.

Gradually the tenement house faded and became a blur before Miss Terry's eyes. Once more she saw the mantelshelf before her and the Christmas angel with outstretched arms waving to and fro. "You see!" he said. "You did not guess all the pleasure that was shut up in that box with old Jack, did you?"

Miss Terry shook her head.

"And you see how different it all was from what you thought. Now let us see what became of the Canton-flannel dog."

"The Flanton dog." Miss Terry amended the phrase under her breath. It seemed so natural to use Tom's word.

"Yes, the Flanton dog," the angel smiled. "What do you think became of him?"

"I saw what became of him," said Miss Terry. "Bob Cooper threw him under an automobile, and he was crushed flatter than a pancake."

"Then you left the window," said the angel. "In your human way you assumed that this was the end. But wait and see."

Once more the room darkened and blurred, and Miss Terry looked out upon past events as upon a busy, ever-shifting stage.

CHAPTER 9

THE DOG AGAIN

HE saw the snowy street, into which, from the tip of his stick, Bob Cooper had just tossed the Flanton dog. She saw, what she had not seen before, the woman and child on the opposite side of the street. She saw the baby stretch out wistful hands after the dog lying in the snow. Then an automobile honked past, and she felt again the thrill of horror as it ran over the poor old toy. At the same moment the child screamed, and she saw it point tearfully at the Flanton tragedy. The mother, who had seen nothing of all this, stopped and spoke to him reprovingly.

"What's the matter, Johnnie?" she said. "Sh! Don't make such a noise. Here we are at Mrs. Wales's gate, and you mustn't make a fuss. Now be a good boy and wait here till Mother comes out."

She rang the area bell and stood, basket in hand, waiting to be admitted. But Johnnie gazed at one spot in the street, with eyes full of tears, and with now and then a sob gurgling from his throat. He could not forget what he had seen.

The door opened for the mother, who disappeared inside the house, with one last command to the child: "Now be a good boy, Johnnie. I'll be back in half a minute."

Hardly was she out of sight when Johnnie started through the snowdrift toward the middle of the street. With difficulty he lifted his little legs out of the deep snow; now and then he stumbled and fell into the soft mass. But he rose only the more determined upon his errand, and kept his eyes fixed on the wreck of the Flanton dog.

Bob Cooper, who was idly strolling up and down the block, smoking a cigarette, as he watched the flitting girlish shadows in a certain window opposite, saw the child's frantic struggles in the snow and was intensely amused. "Bah Jove!" he chuckled. "I believe he's after the wretched dawg that I tossed over there with my stick. Fahncy it!" And carelessly he puffed a whiff of smoke.

At last the baby boy reached the middle of the street and stooped to pick up the battered toy. It was flattened and shapeless, but the child clasped it tenderly and began to coo softly to it.

"Bah Jove!" repeated Cooper. "Fahncy caring so much about anything! Poor kid! Perhaps that is all the Christmas he will have." He blew a thoughtful puff through his nose. "Christmas Eve!" The thought flashed through his mind with a new appeal.

Just then came a sudden *"Honk, honk!"* An automobile had turned the corner and was coming up at full speed. It was the same machine which had passed a few minutes earlier in the opposite direction.

"Hi there!" Cooper yelled to the child. But the latter was sitting in the snow in the middle of the street, rocking back and forth, with the Flanton dog in his arms. There was scarcely time for action. Bob dropped his cigarette and his cane, made one leap into the street and another to the child, and by the impact of his body threw the baby into the drift at the curb. With a horrified *honk* the automobile passed over the young man, who lay senseless in the snow.

He was not killed. Miss Terry saw him taken to his home close by, where his broken leg was set and his bruises attended to. She saw him lying bandaged and white on his bed when the woman and her child were brought to see him. Johnnie was still clasping closely the unlucky Flanton dog.

"Well, kid," said the young man feebly, "so you saved the dog, after all."

"Oh sir!" cried the poor woman, weeping. "Only to think that he would not be here now but for you. What a Christmas that would have been for me! You were so good, so brave!"

"Oh, rot!" protested Bob faintly. "Had to do it; my fault anyway; Christmas Eve—couldn't see a kid hurt on Christmas Eve."

He called the attendant and asked for the pocketbook which had been in his coat at the time of the accident. Putting it into the woman's hand, he said, "Good-bye. Get Johnnie something really jolly for Christmas. I'm afraid the dog is about all in. Get him a new one."

But Johnnie refused to have a new dog. It was the poor, shapeless Flanton animal which remained the darling of his heart for many a year.

BOB COOPER SAVES THE BABY

All this of past and future Miss Terry knew through the angel's power. When once more the library lightened, and she saw the pink figure smiling at her from the mantel, she spoke of her own accord.

"It was my fault, because I put the dog in the way. I caused all that trouble."

"Trouble?" said the angel, puzzled. "Do you call it *trouble?* Do you not see what it has done for that heartless youth? It brought his good moment. Perhaps he will be a different man after this. And as for the child; he was made happy by something that would otherwise have been wasted, and he has gained a friend who will not forget him. Trouble! And do you think *you* did it?" He laughed knowingly.

"I certainly did," said Miss Terry firmly.

"But it was I, yes *I*, the Christmas spirit, who put it into your head to do what you did. You may not believe it, but so it was. You too, even you, Angelina, could not quite escape the influence of the Christmas spirit, and so these things have happened. But now let us see what became of the third experiment."

Chapter 10

NOAH AGAIN

N the street of candles a woman dressed all in black had picked up the poor old Noah's ark and was looking at it wildly. She was a widow who had just lost her only child, a little son, and she was in a state of morbid bitterness bordering on distraction.

When the second woman with the two little ones came up and begged for the toy, something hard and sullen and cruel rose in the widow's heart, and she refused angrily to give up the thing. She hated those two boys who had been spared when her own was taken. She would not make them happy.

"No, you shall not have it" she cried, clutching the Noah's ark fiercely. "I will destroy it."

The poor woman and the children followed her wistfully. The little boys were crying. They were cold and hungry and disappointed. They had come so near to something pleasant. They had almost been lucky; but the luck had passed over their heads to another.

The woman in mourning strode on rapidly, the thoughts within her no less black than the garments which she wore. She hated the world; she hated the people who lived in it. She hated Christmastime, when everyone seemed merry except herself. And yes, yes! Most of all she hated children. She clenched her teeth wickedly; her mind reeled.

Suddenly, somewhere, a chorus of happy voices began to sing the words of an old carol: —

"Holy night! Peaceful night!
All is dark save the light,
Yonder where they sweet vigil keep,

O'er the Babe who in silent sleep
Rests in heavenly peace."

Softly and sweetly the childish voices ascended from the street. The woman in black stopped short, breathing hard. She saw the band of choristers standing in a group on the sidewalk and in the snow, their hats pulled down over their eyes, their collars turned up around their ears, their hands deep in pockets. In their midst rose the tall wooden cross carried by a little fellow with yellow hair. They sang as simply and as heartily as a flock of birds out in the snow.

The woman gave a great sob. Her little lad had been a choirboy—perhaps these were his one-time comrades. The second verse of the carol rang out sweetly:

"Holy night! Peaceful night!
Only for shepherds' sight
Came blest visions of angel throngs,
With their loud Hallelujah songs,
Saying, Jesus is come!"

Suddenly it seemed to the distracted mother that her own boy's voice blended with those others. He too was singing in honor of that Child. Happy and ever young, he was bidding her rejoice in the day which made all childhood sacred. And for his sake she had been hating children!

With a sudden revulsion of feeling she turned to see what had become of the poor mother and her boys. They were not far behind, huddling in the shadow. The black-cloaked woman strode quickly up to them. They shrank pitifully at her approach, and she felt the shame of it. They were afraid of her!

"Here," she said, thrusting the Noah's ark into the hands of the larger boy. "Take it. It belongs to you."

The child took it timidly. The mother began to protest thanks. Trying to control the shake in her voice, the dark lady spoke again. "Have you prepared a Christmas for your children?"

The woman shook her heard. "I have nothing," she sighed. "A roof over our heads, that's all."

"Your husband?"

"He died a month ago."

So other folk had raw sorrows, too. The mourner had forgotten that.

"There is no one expecting you at home?" Again the woman shook her head dolefully. "Come with me," said the dark lady impulsively. "You shall be my guests tonight. And tomorrow I will make a Christmas for the children. The house shall put off its shadow. I too will light candles. I have toys,"—her voice broke—"and clothing; many things, which are being wasted. That is not right! Something led you to me, or me to you; something—perhaps it was an angel—whoever dropped that Noah's ark in the street. An angel might do that, I believe. Come with me."

The woman and her son followed her, rejoicing greatly in the midst of their wonder.

There were tears in the eyes through which Miss Terry saw once more the Christmas angel. She wiped them hastily. But still the angel seemed to shine with a fairer radiance.

"You see!" was all he said. And Miss Terry bowed her head. She began to understand.

Chapter 11

MIRANDA AGAIN

NCE more, on the wings of vision, Miss Terry was out in the snowy street. She was following the fleet steps of a little girl who carried a white-paper package under her arm. Miss Terry knew that she was learning the fate of her old doll, Miranda, whom her own hands had thrust out into a cold world.

Poor Miranda! After all these years to become the property of a thief! Mary was the little thief's name. Hugging the tempting package close, Mary ran and ran until she was out of breath. Her one thought was to get as far as possible from the place where the bundle had lain. For she suspected that the steps where she had found it led up to the doll's home. That was why in her own eyes also she was a little thief. But now she had run so far and had turned so many corners that she could not find her way back if she would. There was triumph in the thought. Mary chuckled to herself as she stopped running and began to walk leisurely in the neighborhood with which she was more familiar.

She pinched the package gently. Yes, there could be no doubt about it. It was a doll—not a very large doll; but Mary reflected that she had never thought she would care for a large doll. Undoubtedly it was a very nice one. Had she not found it in a wealthy part of the city, on the steps of a mansion? Mary gloated over the doll as she fancied it; with real hair, and eyes that opened and shut; with four little white teeth, and hands with dimples in the knuckles. She had seen such dolls in the windows of the big shops. But she had never hoped to have one for her very own.

"Maybe it will have on a blue silk dress and white kid shoes, like that one I saw this morning!" she mused rapturously.

She pinched the spot where she fancied the doll's feet ought to be.

"Yes, she's got shoes, sure enough! I bet they're white, too. They *feel* white. Oh, what fun I shall have with her,"—she hugged the doll fondly—"if Uncle and Aunt don't take her away!"

The sudden thought made her stand still in horror. "They sold Mother's little clock for rum," she said bitterly. "They sold the ring with the red stone that Father gave me on my birthday when I was seven. They sold the presents that I got at Sunday school last year. Oh, wouldn't it be dreadful it they should sell my new doll! And I know they will want to if they see her." She squeezed the bundle closer with the prescient pang of parting.

"Maybe they'll be out somewhere." With this faint hope she reached the tenement and crept up the dingy stairs. She peeped in at the door. Alas! Her uncle and aunt were in the kitchen, through which she had to pass. They had company; some dirty-looking men and women, and there were a jug and glasses on the table before them. Mary's heart sank, but she nodded bravely to the company and tried to slip through the crowd to the other room. But her aunt was quick to see that she carried something under her coat.

"What you got there? A Christmas present?" she sneered.

Mary flushed. "No," she said slowly, "just something I found."

"Found? Hello, what is it? A package!"

Her uncle advanced and snatched it from her.

"Please," pleaded Mary, "please, I found it. It is mine. I think it is only a doll."

"A doll! Huh! Who needs a doll?" hiccoughed her uncle. "We want something more to drink. We'll sell it—"

A bellow of laughter resounded through the room. The paper being torn roughly away, poor Miranda stood revealed in all her faded beauty. The pallid waxen face, straggling hair, and old-fashioned dress presented a sorry sight to the greedy eyes which had expected to find something exchangeable for drink. A sorry sight she was to Mary, who had hoped for something so much lovelier. A flush of disappointment came into her cheek, and tears to her eyes.

"Here, take your old doll," said her uncle roughly, thrusting it into her arms. "Take your old doll and get away with her. If that's the best you can find you'd better *steal* something next time."

Steal something! Had she not in fact stolen it? Mary knew very well that she had, and she flushed pinker yet to think what a fool she had made of herself for nothing. She took the despised doll and retreated into the other room, followed by a chorus of jeers and comments. She banged the door behind her and sat down with poor Miranda on her knees, crying as if her heart would break. She had so longed for a beautiful doll! It did seem too cruel that when she found one it should turn out to be so ugly. She seized poor Miranda and shook her fiercely.

"You horrid old thing!" she said. "Ain't you ashamed to fool me so? Ain't you ashamed to make me think you was a lovely doll with pretty clothes and *white kid shoes?* Ain't you?"

She shook Miranda again until her eyeballs rattled in her head. The doll fell to the floor and lay there with closed eyes. Her face was pallid and ghastly. Her bonnet had fallen off, and her hair stuck out wildly in every direction. Her legs were doubled under her in the most helpless fashion. She was the forlornest figure of a doll imaginable. Presently Mary drew her hands away from her eyes and looked down at Miranda. There was something in the doll's attitude as she lay there which touched the little girl's heart. Once she had seen a woman who had been injured in the street—she would never forget it. The poor creature's eyes had been closed, and her face, under the fallen bonnet, was of this same pasty color. Mary shuddered. Suddenly she felt a warm rush of pity for the doll.

"You poor old thing!" she exclaimed, looking at Miranda almost tenderly. "I'm sorry I shook you. You look so tired and sad and homesick! I wonder if somebody is worrying about you this minute. It was very wicked of me to take you away—on Christmas Eve, too! I wish I had left you where I found you. Maybe some little girl is crying now because you are lost."

Mary stooped and lifted the doll gently upon her knees. As she took Miranda up, the blue eyes opened and seemed to look full at her. Miranda's one beauty was her eyes. Mary felt her heart grow warmer and warmer toward the quaint stranger.

"You have lovely eyes," she murmured. "I think after all you are almost pretty. Perhaps I should grow to like you awfully. You are not a bit like the doll I hoped to have; but that is not your fault." A thought made her face brighten. *Why, if you had been a beautiful doll they would have taken you away and sold you for rum.* Her face expressed utter disgust. She hugged Miranda close with a sudden outburst of affection. "Oh, you dear old thing!" she cried. "I am so glad you are—just like this. I am so glad, for now I can keep you always and always, and no one will want to take you away from me."

She rocked to and fro, holding the doll tightly to her heart. Mary was not one to feel a half passion about anything. "I will make you some new dresses," she said, fingering the old-fashioned silk with a puzzled air. "I wonder why your mother dressed you so queerly? She was not much of a sewer if she made this bonnet!" Scornfully she took off the primitive bonnet and smoothed out the tangled hair. "I wonder what you have on underneath," she said.

With gentle fingers she began to undress Miranda. Off came the green silk dress with its tight basque and overskirt. Off came the ruffled petticoat and little chemise edged with fine lace. And Miranda stood in shapeless, kid-bodied ugliness, which stage of evolution the doll of her day had reached.

But there was something more. Around her neck she wore a ribbon; on the ribbon was a cardboard medal; and on the medal a childish hand had scratched these words:

Miranda Terry.
If lost, please return her to her mother,
Angelina Terry,
87 Overlook Terrace.

It was such a card as Miss Terry herself had worn in the days when her mother had first let her and Tom go out to the street without a nurse.

Mary stared hard at the bit of cardboard. Eighty-seven Overlook Terrace! Yes, that was where she had found the doll. She remembered now seeing the name on a street corner. *Miranda;* what a pretty name for a doll! *Angelina Terry;* so that was the name of the little girl who had lost Miranda. Angelina must be feeling very sorry now. Perhaps she was crying herself to sleep, for it was growing late.

Her two girl cousins came romping into the bedroom. They had been having a hilarious evening.

"Hello, Mary!" they cried. "We heard about your great find!"—"Playing with your old doll, are you? Goin' to hang up her stockin' and see if Santa Claus will fill it?"—"Huh! Santa Claus won't come to *this* house, I guess!"

Mary had almost forgotten that it was Christmas Eve. There had been nothing in the house to remind her. Perhaps Angelina Terry had hung up a stocking for Miranda at 87 Overlook Terrace. But there would be no Miranda to see it the next morning.

Her cousins teased her for some time, while they undressed, and Mary grew sulky. She sat in her corner and said very little. But eventually the room grew quiet, for the girls slept easily. Then Mary crept into her little cot with the doll in her arms. She loved Miranda so much that she would never part with her, no indeed; not even though she now knew where Miranda belonged. Eighty-seven Overlook Terrace! The figures danced before her eyes maliciously. She wished she could forget them. And the thought of Angelina Terry kept coming to her. Poor Angelina!

She ain't "poor Angelina," argued Mary to herself. *She's rich Angelina. Doesn't she live in a big house in the swell part of the city? I s'pose she has hundreds of dolls, much handsomer than Miranda, and lots of other toys. I guess she won't miss this one queer old doll. I guess she'd let me keep it if she knew I hadn't any of my own. I guess it ought to be my doll. Anyway, I'm going to keep her. I don't believe Angelina loves Miranda so much as I do.*

She laid her cheek against the doll's cold waxen one and presently fell asleep.

But she slept uneasily. In the middle of the night she awoke and lay for hours tossing and unhappy in the stuffy little room. The clock struck one, two, three. At last she gave a great sigh, and cuddling Miranda in her arms turned over, with peace in her heart.

"I will play you are mine, my very own dollie, for just this one night," she whispered in Miranda's ear. "Tomorrow will be Christmas Day, and I will take you back to your little mother, Angelina Terry. I can't do a mean thing at Christmastime—not even for you, dear Miranda."

Thereupon she fell into a peaceful sleep.

Chapter 12

The Angel Again

ILL she bring it back?" asked Miss Terry eagerly, when once more she found herself under the gaze of the Christmas angel. He nodded brightly.

"Tomorrow morning you will see," he said. "It will prove that all I have shown you is really true."

"A pretty child," said Miss Terry musingly. "A very nice child indeed. I believe she looks very much as I used to be myself."

"You see, she is not a thief after all; not *yet,"* said the angel. "What a pity that she must live in that sad home, with such terrible people! A sensitive child like her, craving sympathy and affection—what chance has she for happiness? What would you yourself have been in surroundings like hers?"

"Yes, she is very like what I was. Of course I shall let her keep the doll."

Miss Terry hesitated. The angel looked at her steadily and his glance seemed to read her half-formed thoughts.

"Surely," he said. "It seems to belong to her, does it not? But is this all? I wonder if something more does not belong to her."

"What more?" asked Miss Terry shortly.

"A home!" cried the angel.

Miss Terry groped in her memory for a scornful retort which she had once been fond of using, but there was no such word to be found. Instead there came to her lips the name, "Mary."

The angel repeated it softly, "*Mary.* It is a blessed name," he said. "Blessed the roof that shelters a Mary in her need."

There was a long silence, in which Miss Terry felt new impulses stirring within her; impulses drawing her to the child whose looks recalled her own childhood. The angel regarded her with beaming eyes. After some time he said quietly, "Now let us see what became of your last experiment."

Miss Terry started. It seemed as if she had been interrupted in pleasant dreaming. "*You* were the last experiment," she said. "I knew what became of you. Here you are!"

"Yet more have happened than you guessed," replied the angel meaningfully. "I have tried to show you how often that is the case. Look again."

Without moving from her chair Miss Terry seemed to be looking out on her sidewalk, where, so it seemed, she had just laid the pink figure of the angel. She saw the drunken man approach. She heard his coarse laugh; saw his brutal movement as he kicked the Christmas symbol into the street. In sick disgust she saw him reel away out of sight. She saw herself run down the steps, rescue the angel, and bring it into the house. Surely the story was finished. What more could there be?

But something bade her vision follow the steps of the wretched man. Down the street he reeled, singing a blasphemous song. With a whoop he rounded a corner and ran into a happy party which filled sidewalk and street, as it hurried in the direction from which he came. Good-naturedly they jostled him against the wall, and he grasped a railing to steady himself as they swept by. It was the choir on their way to carol in the next street. Before them went the cross-bearer, lifting high his simple wooden emblem.

The eyes of the drunken man caught sight of this, and wavered. The presence of the crowd conveyed no meaning to his dazed brains. But there was something in the familiar symbol which held his vision. He looked, and crossed himself, remembering the traditions of his childhood. Some of the boys were humming, as they went, the stirring strains of an ancient Christmas march known to all nations; a carol which began, some say, as a rousing drinking chorus.

The familiar strain touched some chord in the sodden brain. The man gave a feeble whinny, trying to follow the melody. He pulled himself together and lurched forward in a sudden impulse to join the band of pilgrims. But by the time he had taken three steps they had vanished, miraculously, as it seemed to him.

"Begorra, they're gone!" he cried. "Who were they? Were they rale folks? What was it they was singin'?"

He sank back helplessly on a flight of steps. *"Ve-ni-te a-do-re-mus!"* he croaked in a quavering basso. And his tangled mind went through strange

HE GRASPED A RAILING TO STEADY HIMSELF

processes. Suddenly, there came to him in a flash of exaggerated memory the figure of the Christmas angel which not ten minutes earlier he had kicked into the street. A pious horror fell upon him.

"Mither o' mercy!" he cried, again crossing himself. "What have I been an' done? It was a howly image; an' what did I do to ut? Lemme go back an' find ut, an' take ut up out av the street."

Greatly sobered by his fear, he staggered down the block and around the corner to the steps of Miss Terry's house.

"This is the place," he mused. "I know ut; here's where the frindly lam'post hild me in its arrums. I rimimber there was a dark house forninst me. Here's where ut lay on the sidewalk, all pink an' pretty. An' I kicked ut into the street! Where is ut now? Where gone? Howly Mither! Here's the spot where ut fell, look now! The shape of uts little body and the wings of ut in the snow. But 'tis gone intirely!" He rubbed his eyes and crossed himself again. "'Tis flown away," he muttered. "'Tis gone back to hiven to tell Mary Mither o' the wicked thing I done this night. Oh, 'tis a miracle that's happened! An' oh! The wicked man I am, drunk and disorderly on the howly eve!"

"O come, all ye faithful,
Joyful and triumphant!"

Once more he heard the familiar strain taken up lustily by many voices.

"Hear all the world singin' on the way to Bethlehem!" he said, and the stupor seemed to leave his brain. He no longer staggered.

"I'll run an' join 'em, an' I won't drink another drop this night." He looked up at the starry sky. "Maybe the angel hears me. Maybe he'll help me to keep straight tomorrow. It might be my guardian angel himself that I treated so! Saints forgive me!"

With head bowed humbly, but no longer reeling, he moved away towards the sound of music.

"You were his guardian angel," said Miss Terry, when once more she saw the figure on the mantelshelf. And she spoke with reverent gentleness.

The angel smiled brightly. "The Christmas spirit is a guardian angel to many," he said. "Never again despise me, Angelina. Never again make light of my influence."

"Never again," murmured Miss Terry half unconsciously. "I wish it were not too late—"

"It is never too late," said the Christmas angel eagerly, as if he read her unspoken thought. "Oh, never too late, Angelina."

Chapter 13

THE CHRISTMAS CANDLE

UDDENLY there was a sound—a dull reverberating sound. It seemed to Miss Terry to come from neither north, south, east, nor west, but from a different world. Ah! She recognized it now. It was somebody knocking on the library door.

Miss Terry gave a long sigh and drew herself up in her chair. "It must be Norah just come back," she said to herself. "I had forgotten Norah completely. It must be shockingly late. Come in," she called, as she glanced at the clock.

She rubbed her eyes and looked again. A few minutes after nine! She had thought it must be midnight!

Norah entered to find her mistress staring at the mantel where the clock stood. She saw lying beside the clock the pink angel which had fallen from the box as she brought it in—the box now empty by the fire.

"Law, Miss," she said, "have you burned them all up but him? I'm glad you saved him, he's so pretty."

"Norah," said Miss Terry with an effort, "is that clock right?"

"Yes'm," said Norah. "I set it this morning. I came back as soon as I could, Miss," she added apologetically.

"It isn't that," answered Miss Terry, drawing her hand across her forehead dazedly. "I did not mind your absence. But I thought it must be later."

"Oh, no, I wouldn't stay out any later when you was alone here, Miss," said Norah penitently. "I felt ashamed after I had gone. I ought not to have left you so—on Christmas Eve. But oh, Miss! The singing was so beautiful, and the houses looked so grand with the candles in the windows. It is like a holy night indeed!"

Miss Terry stooped and picked up something from the floor. It was the bit of candle-end which had escaped the holocaust.

"Are the candles still lighted, Norah?" she asked, eyeing the bit of wax in her hand.

"Yes'm, some of them," answered the maid. "It is getting late, and a good many have burned out. But some houses are still as bright as ever."

"Perhaps it is not too late, then," murmured Miss Terry, as if yielding a disputed point. "Let us hurry, Norah."

She rose, and going to the mantelshelf gently took up the figure of the angel, while Norah looked on in amazement.

"Norah," said Miss Terry, with an eagerness which made her voice tremble, "I want you to hang the Christmas angel in the window there. I too have a fancy to burn a candle tonight. If it is not too late I'd like to have a little share in the Christmas spirit."

Norah's eyes lighted. "Oh, yes'm," she said. "I'll hang it right away. And I'll find an empty spool to hold the candle."

She bustled briskly about, and presently in the window appeared a little device unlike any other in the block. Against the darkness within, the figure of the angel with arms outstretched towards the street shone in a soft light from the flame of a single tiny candle such as blossom on Christmas trees.

It caught the attention of many home-goers, who said, smiling, "How simple! How pretty! How quaint! It is a type of the Christmas spirit which is abroad tonight. You can feel it everywhere, blessing the city."

For some minutes before the candle was lighted, a man muffled in a heavy overcoat had been standing in a doorway opposite Miss Terry's house. He was tall and grizzled and his face was sad. He stared up at the gloomy windows, the only oblongs of blackness in the illuminated block, and he shivered, shrugging his shoulders.

"The same as ever!" he said to himself. "I might have known she would never change. Anyone else, on Christmas Eve, after the letter I wrote her, would have softened a little. But I might have known. She is hard as nails! Of course, it was my fault in the first place to leave her as I did. But when I acknowledged it, and when I wrote that letter on Christmas Eve, I thought Angelina might feel differently." He looked at his watch. "Nearly half past nine," he muttered. "I may as well go home. She said she wanted to be let alone; that Christmas meant nothing to her. I don't dare to call—on my only sister! I suppose she is there all alone, and here I am all alone, too. What a pity! If I saw the least sign—"

Just then there was the spark of a match against the darkness framed in by the window opposite. A hand and arm shone in the flicker of light across the upper sash. A tiny spark, tremulous at first, like a bird alighting on a frail branch, paused, steadied, and became fixed. In the light of a small taper the man caught a glimpse of a pale, long face in a frame of silver hair. It faded into the background. But above the candle he now saw, with arms outstretched it seemed toward himself, a pink little angel with gauzy wings.

The man's heart gave a leap. Sudden memories thronged his brain, making him almost dizzy. At last they formulated into one smothered cry. "*The Christmas angel!* It is the very same pink angel that Angelina and I used to hang on our Christmas tree!"

In three great leaps, like a schoolboy, he crossed the street and ran up the steps of number 87. The Christmas angel seemed to smile with ineffable sweetness as he gave the bell a vigorous pull.

Chapter 14

TOM

MISS Terry was leaning on the mantelshelf looking into the fire, when the bell pealed furiously. She started and turned pale.

"Lord 'a' mercy!" responded Norah, who was still admiring the effect of the window decoration. "What's that? Who can be calling here tonight, making such a noise?"

"Go to the door, Norah," said Miss Terry with a strange note in her voice. "It may be someone to see me. It is not too late."

"Yes'm," said Norah, obedient but bewildered.

Presently the library door opened and a figure strode in; a tall, broad-shouldered man in a fur overcoat. For a moment he stood just inside the door, hesitating. Miss Terry took two steps forward from the fireplace.

"Tom!" she said faintly. "You came—after all!"

"After all, Angelina," he said. "Yes, because I saw *that,"* he waved his hand toward the window. "That gave me courage to come in. It is our Christmas angel. I remember all about it. Does it mean anything, Angelina?"

Miss Terry held out a moment longer. Then she faltered forward. "Oh, Tom!" she sobbed, as she felt his brotherly, strong arms about her. "Oh, Tom! And so he has brought you back to me, and me to you!"

"He? Angelina girl, who?" He smoothed her silver hair with rough, kind fingers.

"Why, the Christmas angel; our guardian angel, Tom. All these years I kept him in the play box, and I was going to burn him up. But I couldn't do it, Tom. How wonderful it is!"

They sat down before the fire and she began to tell him the whole story. But she interrupted herself to send for Norah, who came to her, mystified and half scandalized by the greeting which she had seen those two oldsters exchange.

"This is my brother Tom, Norah, who has come back," she said. "I believe it is not too late to make some preparation for Christmas Day. The stores will still be open. Run out and order things for a grand occasion, Norah. And—oh, Norah!" a sudden remembrance came to her. "If you have time, will you please get some toys and pretty things such as a little girl would like; a little girl of about ten, with my complexion—I mean, with yellow hair and blue eyes. We may have a little guest tomorrow."

"Yes'm," said Norah, moving like one in a dream.

"A guest?" exclaimed Tom. And Miss Terry told him about Mary.

"I love little girls," said Tom, "especially little girls with yellow hair and blue eyes, such as you used to have, Angelina."

"You will like Mary, then," said Miss Terry, with a pretty pink flush of pleasure in her cheeks.

"I shall like her, *if* she comes," amended Tom, who, man-like, received with reservations the account of a vision vouchsafed not unto him.

"She will come," said Miss Terry with her old positiveness, glancing towards the window where the Christmas angel hung.

Then arose the sound of singing outside the house. The passing choristers had spied the quaint window, now the only one in the street which remained lighted:

"When Christ was born of Mary free,
In Bethlehem, in that fair citye,
Angels sang with mirth and glee,
In Excelsis Gloria!"

Chapter 15

CHRISTMAS DAY

ND Mary came. The brother and sister were at breakfast—the happiest which either of them had known for years—when there came a timid pull at the front-door bell. Miss Angelina laid down her knife and fork and looked across the table at Tom.

"She has come. Mary has come," she said. "Norah, if it is a little girl with a package under her arm, bring her in here."

"Yes'm!" gasped Norah, who believed she was living in a dream where everything was topsy-turvy. When had a child last entered Miss Terry's dining room!

Norah disappeared and presently returned ushering in a little girl of ten, with blue eyes and yellow hair. Under her arm she carried a white-paper package, very badly wrapped.

Miss Terry exchanged with her brother a glance which said, *I told you so!*

The child seemed bashful and afraid to speak; no wonder!

Tom's kind heart yearned to her. "Good morning! We wish you a merry Christmas, Mary!" he said smiling.

The child gave a start. "Why, how did you know my name?" she cried.

Tom looked confused. How indeed did he know? But Miss Angelina, with a readiness that surprised herself, came to his rescue.

"We were talking of a little girl named Mary," she said. "And you look just like her. What did you come for, dear?"

The little girl hung her head and turned crimson.

"I—I came to see Angelina Terry," she whispered. "I—I've got a doll that belongs to her."

There was a pause, then Miss Terry said, "Well, go on."

"I—I found her on the steps of this house last night, and I ought to have brought her right here then. But I didn't. I took her home. I hope Angelina was not very unhappy last night."

Miss Terry smiled upon Tom, who gave a kind, low laugh.

"No," said Miss Terry. "Angelina did not worry about her lost doll. She was thinking about something else—the nicest Christmas present that ever anybody had. But you were a good girl to bring back the doll."

"No, I'm not a good girl," said Mary, and her voice trembled. "I was a wicked girl. I meant to keep Miranda for myself, because I thought she would be a lovely big doll. And when I found she was old and homely, somehow I still wanted to keep her. But it was stealing, and I couldn't. Please, will you give her to Angelina, and tell her I am so sorry?" She took Miranda out of the wrapping and held her toward Miss Terry without looking at the doll. It was as if she were afraid of being tempted once more.

Miss Terry did not take the doll.

"I am Angelina," she said. "The doll was mine."

"You! Angelina!" the child's face was full of bewilderment. Mechanically she drew Miranda to her and clasped her close.

"Yes, I am Angelina, and that was my doll Miranda," said Miss Terry gently. "Thank you for returning her. But Mary—your name *is* Mary?" The child nodded. "Suppose I wanted you to keep her for me, what would you say?"

Mary's eyes still dwelt upon Miss Terry with a puzzled look. This gray-haired Angelina was so different from the one she had pictured. She did not answer the question. Miss Terry drew the child to a chair beside her.

"Tell me all about yourself, Mary," she said.

After some coaxing and prompting from what they already guessed, Mary told the story of her sad little life.

She was an orphan recently left to the care of her uncle and aunt, who had received her grudgingly. They were her sole relatives, and the shame of their degraded lives was plain through the outlines of the vague picture which Mary sketched of them.

"You do not love them, Mary?" asked Miss Terry kindly.

"No," answered the child. "They always speak crossly to me. When they have been drinking they beat me."

Tom rose from the table with a muttered word and began to pace the floor. His blue eyes were full of tears.

"Mary," said Miss Terry, "will the people at home be worried if you do not come back to dinner?"

MARY RETURNS THE DOLL

Mary shook her head wonderingly. "No," she said. "They will not care. I am often away on holidays. I go to the museums."

"Then I want you to stay with us today," said Miss Terry. "We are going to have a Christmas celebration, and we need you for a guest. Will you stay, you and Miranda?"

Mary looked down at the doll in her arms, and up at the two kind faces bent toward her. "Yes," she said impulsively, "I will stay. How good you are! I don't want to go home."

"Don't go home!" burst out Tom. "Stay with us always and be our little girl."

Mary looked from one to the other, half frightened at the new idea. Miss Terry bent and pecked at her cheek, with a thrill at the new sensation.

"Yes, we mean it," she said, and her voice was almost sweet. "We believe that the Christmas angel has brought you to us, Mary. You have the Christmas name. But you seem to us like the little girl we both knew best, little Angelina with blue eyes and yellow hair, who was Miranda's mother. Will you stay with us, Mary Angelina? Would you like to stay?

Mary looked up with a wistful smile. "You are so good!" she said again. "I wish I could stay. But Uncle and Aunt are so—I am afraid of what they might do to us all. If they thought you wanted me, they would not let me go."

"I will fix Uncle and Aunt," said Tom, going for his coat. "Leave them to me. I know an argument that settles uncles and aunts of that sort. You need not go back to their house, I promise you, Mary, my dear."

Mary gave a great sigh of relief. "Oh, I am so glad!" she said. "It was such a wicked house. And here it is so good!"

"Good!" Miss Terry echoed the word with a sigh. "Come with me, Mary," she said.

She led her little guest through the hall to the library, where a great fire was blazing, with sundry mysterious packages in white paper piled on the table beside it. But Miss Terry did not stop at the fireplace. She drew Mary to the window which looked out on the sidewalk. Above the lower sash Mary saw the remains of a burned-out Christmas candle; and over it hung a pink papier-mâché angel stretching out open arms toward her.

"This is the Christmas angel, Mary," said Miss Terry. "He is as old as Miranda—"

"He is as old as Christmas," interrupted Tom, looking in from the hall.

"When we were children, Tom and I, we hung him on our Christmas tree," went on Miss Terry. "We think he brought you to us. We believe he has changed the world for us—has brought us peace, goodwill, and happiness. He is going to be the guardian angel of our house. You must love him, Mary."

"How beautiful he is!" said Mary reverently. "His face shines like the Baby's that I saw once in the church. Oh, Miss Angelina! He is like the Christ Child himself!"

"Call me Aunt Angelina," said Miss Terry with a quick breath.

"Aunt Angelina," cried the child, throwing her arms about Miss Terry's neck.

Tom came and put his great furry coat-sleeves about them both. "And Uncle Tom," he said.

"Dear Uncle Tom!" whispered the child shyly.

There were tears in the eyes of all three.

"Now we shall live happy ever after," said Tom.

And the Christmas angel beamed upon them.

Afterword

Discussion with Professor Wheeler

(For Formal School, Home School, and Book Club Discussions)

First of all, permit me to define my perception of the role of the teacher. I believe that the ideal teaching relationship involves the teacher and the student, both looking in the same direction, and both having a sense of wonder. A teacher is *not* an important person dishing out rote learning to an unimportant person. I furthermore do not believe that a Ph.D. automatically brings with it omniscience, despite the way some of us act. In discussions, I tell my students beforehand that my opinions and conclusions are no more valid than theirs, for each of us sees reality from a different perspective.

Now that my role is clear, let's continue. The purpose of the discussion sections of the series is to encourage debate, to dig deeper into the books than would be true without these sections, and to spawn other questions that may build on the ones I begin with. If you take advantage of these sections, you will be gaining just as good an understanding of a book as you would were you actually sitting in one of my classroom circles.

As you read this book, record your thoughts and reactions each day in a journal. Also, an unabridged dictionary is almost essential in completely understanding the text. If your vocabulary is to grow, something else is needed besides the dictionary: vocabulary cards. Take a stack of three-by-five-inch cards, and write the words you don't know on one side and their definitions on the other, with each word used in a sentence. Every time you stumble on words you are unsure of—and I found quite a number myself!—make a card for it. Continually go over these cards; and keep all, except those you never miss, in a card file. You will be amazed at how fast your vocabulary will grow!

The Introduction Must Be Read Before Beginning the Next Section.

- - -

Questions to Deepen Your Understanding

Chapter 1. The Play Box

1. Beginning sentences and paragraphs often make or break a book. In this book, Abbie Farwell Brown drops us right into dialogue and action in progress. What does this first paragraph accomplish, in terms of your desire to read on, or to close the book and leave the rest of the book unread?

2. Pay particular attention to how Brown fleshes out her characters. On five-by-eight-inch cards (one for each character in the book), chart out the evolution of each character, starting with Miss Terry and Norah. First impressions (both in real life and in literature) are so powerful that they might as well be carved in marble. Flat characters, as we know, remain frozen in their created state; round characters refuse such imprisonment and smash their way through to freedom. Which characters do you feel are flat in the book? Which round?

   Sometimes we arrive at our initial snap judgment on the basis of what the author says about a given character; and sometimes the author steps back into the shadows and lets the character's words and body language carry their own freight. Which method do you feel works the best? Why?

3. Unquestionably, where Christmas stories and books are concerned, every one of them is compared—consciously or unconsciously—to the great original of the genre, Dickens' 1843 masterpiece, *The Christmas Carol*. Since this is so, start out at the very beginning noting similarities and differences, and weighing their relative effectiveness. In other words, just because a work may achieve icon status, that does not mean that it is therefore immune to all future challenges to its preeminence. Compare the two works. Which one moves you

most deeply? Which one's persuasiveness is harder to resist? Are their methodologies different? Are the two plots similar? Or are there significant differences? Continue to compare through *each chapter*, then arrive at overall conclusions at the book's end.

4. "Alone on Christmas Eve"—What is the impact of that line? Why is it harder to be alone on Christmas Eve than at other times? Or is it?

5. What do you think Miss Terry means by labeling "candles and carols and merriment" as mere superstition? How do her scornful Christmas-related musings compare to Scrooge's in *The Christmas Carol*?

6. Note how the size of Tom's long-ago lettering, compared to her own, only reinforces Miss Terry's determination to have nothing to do with her long-estranged brother. Could it be human nature to skew everything, all evidence, all documentation, in the direction of our predetermined course of action? If that is true, why is it?

7. What is the significance of Miss Terry's first name, in light of the overall story?

8. Old toys today bring small fortunes at antique shows. Is that perceived "value" as significant as the toys' esoteric value? Why?

   Do you agree with Miss Terry's contention that "Most things are better destroyed as soon as you are done with them"? Or do you feel there are valid reasons to hold on to them for purely sentimental reasons? Why?

Chapter 2. Jack-in-the-Box

9. Until recently, houses tended to be lived in by generation after generation of the same families. What would it be like to live in a house that your ancestors had been born in, lived in, and died in? Would you prefer that to shifting from house to house as we do today? What are the benefits of visiting the houses where famous people once lived?

10. Have you ever owned a jack-in-the box? Have you ever wanted to? How do you react to the jack's leaping out of the box?

11. How early do we acquire the urge to possess something? Is it a good trait? A bad trait? Are there any dangers connected with it? Discuss.

12. Does Miss Terry appear to be a bigot? Does she appear to like those of Jewish descent? Since Jews don't believe in Christmas, how does she relate the fighting of the two ragamuffins to that Christian holiday? As the story progresses, watch to see if this initial negative perception persists.

Chapter 3. The Flanton Dog

13. Preconceptions—we all have them. What preconceptions does Miss Terry have about the "dapper figure in a long coat and a silk hat"? Hold them until later in the book so as to see if her preconceptions turn out to be on the mark.

14. Ironic, isn't it, that Miss Terry, who has determined to burn up her old toys, nevertheless feels "a pang shoot through her" as an automobile drives over the battered old toy dog. Can you make sense out of that?

Chapter 4. The Noah's Ark

15. Why is it, do you think, that so few toys survive intact? Are they deliberately mistreated, or does it just "happen"?

16. Prior to our age, when someone died, surviving family wore black as a symbol of mourning, for weeks, months, years—sometimes for life. Do you think we ought to go back to such a tradition? Give reasons.

17. To what perversity in our makeup do we owe our valuing only what others value, desiring only what others desire, and considering as worthless only what others consider worthless? What point is Brown trying to make (with the two women) about human nature? Is this a condition that we can overcome? How?

Chapter 5. Miranda

18. Compare the role Brown's old toys have in her story to that of "real-life" people in Scrooge's youth, in *The Christmas Carol.* Is one device more effective than the other (or only different)? Also study comparative impact on the two protagonists: Ebenezer Scrooge and Angelina Terry.

19. If the eyes are the windows of the soul, what is the effect on Miss Terry of Miranda's eyes? Why would burning her seem like murder? And why did she wrap her in paper when she had failed to do so with the other toys?

20. Why do you feel Miss Terry can now heave the rest of the toys into the fire without any of the reservations she had earlier in the evening's experiments? Would you have felt the same way? Why?

Chapter 6. The Christmas Angel

21. How many of life's troubles, do you think, are caused by our own determination to be first? Why do we insist on such preeminence?

    And when such rivalry once rears its malevolent head among siblings, oftentimes life-long alienation, bitterness, and tragedy is the result, just as it happened between Tom and Angelina. Have you noted similar cases or experienced them yourself? With what results?

22. In what way did Miss Terry feel her mother had been wise fifty years before?

23. Why did Miss Terry rescue the Christmas angel from the muddy street, and why did she find it impossible to toss it into the fire as she had so many other toys?

24. Were you surprised that the Christmas angel was male? Look in the Bible and see what it says about angels being male or female. Why do so many people today assume angels are female?

Chapter 7. Before the Fire

25. What do you think is symbolized by the tradition of placing an angel at the top of each Christmas tree?

26. What do you believe is meant by these words: "Now you have lost the old belief and the old love. . . . Now you have studied books and read wise men's sayings. You understand the higher criticism, and the higher charity, and the higher egoism. You don't believe in mere giving. You don't believe in the Christmas spirit—you know better"?

27. As the story continues, try to gain a concept of the full meaning of "Christmas spirit" as used in the book.

Chapter 8. Jack Again

28. What did Miss Terry learn in the rest of the jack-in-the-box story (especially where appearances and circumstantial evidence are concerned)?

Chapter 9. The Dog Again

29. Why is it, do you think, that toys have greater reality to children than they do to adults? How is that borne out in this chapter?

30. Just as was true of the fabled "velveteen rabbit," Johnnie refuses a new replacement for the battered old dog. Why is it that a child would reject a new and perfect dog, preferring to stay with the crippled old one?

31. All that happens to us is a matter of perspective: We may perceive it as tragic whereas in reality the act may result in wonderful and unexpected things happening to us. How is this truth brought home to Miss Terry?

Chapter 10. Noah Again

32. How difficult it must be to look out from behind bars of pain to people outside who are happy! That is the widow's plight here. Does the reality of her anguish make it easier to forgive her for her selfish act?

33. What role do the carol singers have in this book? How does their singing contribute to the story? Which characters are impacted by it? How?

34. What is your perception of the role of angels in our lives? Do you think an angel might minister through a papier-mâché counterpart?

Chapter 11. Miranda Again

35. What do you think Brown meant by this line? "Once more, on the wings of vision, Miss Terry was out on the snowy street"? Do you

believe a Higher Power may choose to communicate with us through dreams or visions? Have you ever known personally of such communication? Discuss.

36. "Mary was not one to feel a half passion about anything"—what a thing to say! How about you? If you had to choose between a friend known for "half passions" and a friend known for "full passions," which one would you rather have? Why?

37. *Rationalize* is a rather disturbing word. In this chapter, Mary rationalizes for all she's worth to avoid taking Miranda back. Do *we* rationalize? For what reasons? How about you—do you rationalize? If so, are you able to convince your inner self that all is well in spite of it? Is Mary's rationalizing strong enough to convince her questioning conscience? Has your conscience ever kept *you* awake? Discuss.

Chapter 12. The Angel Again

38. What is the significance of the name of the little girl who finds Miranda in this story? Does her name make a difference to Miss Terry?

39. To all appearances, the drunkard who kicked the Christmas angel into the street was a hopeless case, and Miss Terry scorned him. What does she now discover about her snap judgment of him? Do we do this sort of holier-than-thou thing very often? Why? What can we do to change such snap judgments?

Chapter 13. The Christmas Candle

40. How does this section compare to the counterpart in *The Christmas Carol*?

    How much time has passed since Norah left?

41. What is the significance of Angelina Terry's placing the angel in her window?

    What is the significance to the grizzled man watching from across the street?

Chapter 14. Tom

42. How do Angelina's Christmas angel and her guardian angel blur together?

    Does her brother believe her story?

Chapter 15. Christmas Day

43. How does the coming of Mary bring Angelina and Tom full circle?

44. What is the overall impact of the book on you?

45. How effective are the concluding lines?

Coda

Reactions, responses, and suggestions are very important to us. Also, if a particular book—especially an older one—has been loved by you or your family, and you would like to see us incorporate it into this series, drop us a line, with any details about its earliest publisher, printing date, and so on, and send it to

Joe Wheeler, Ph.D.
c/o Focus on the Family
Colorado Springs, CO 80920

About the Editor

Joseph Leininger Wheeler's earliest memories have to do with books and stories—more specifically, of listening to his mother read aloud both in public and to him at home. Wheeler recalls that, as soon as he was able to read, he followed his mother around the house, relentlessly reading his storybooks to her.

Shortly after Wheeler turned eight, his parents moved from California to Latin America as missionaries. From the third through the tenth grade, he was home-schooled by his mother. Of those years, he says today, "I was incredibly lucky and blessed. My mother, a trained teacher and elocutionist, was a voracious reader of books worth reading and had memorized thousands of pages of readings, poetry, and stories. All of that she poured into me. Wherever we went, she encouraged me to devour entire libraries."

At 16, Wheeler returned to California to complete his high school years at Monterey Bay Academy near Santa Cruz. Because of his inherited love of the printed word, Wheeler majored in history at Pacific Union College in the Napa Valley, completing both bachelor's and master's degrees there. After completing a master's in English at California State University in Sacramento, Wheeler attended Vanderbilt University, where he obtained a Ph.D. in English.

Today, after 34 years of teaching at the adult education, college, high school, and junior high levels, Wheeler is Professor Emeritus at Columbia Union College in Takoma Park, Maryland. The world's foremost authority on frontier writer Zane Grey, Wheeler is also the founder and executive director of Zane Grey's West Society and Senior Fellow for Cultural Studies at the Center for the New West in Denver, Colorado. He is editor/compiler of the popular *Christmas in My Heart* series (Review & Herald; Doubleday; Tyndale House); editor/compiler of the story anthologies *Dad in My Heart* and *Mom in My Heart* (Tyndale House); and editor/compiler of Focus on the Family's *Great Stories Remembered* and *Great Stories* series (Tyndale House). Along the way, Wheeler has established nine libraries in schools and colleges, as well as building up his own collection (as large as some college libraries).

Joe Wheeler and his wife, Connie, are the parents of two grown children, Greg and Michelle, and now make their home in Conifer, Colorado.

FOCUS ON THE FAMILY®

Welcome to the Family!

Whether you received this book as a gift, borrowed it from a friend, or purchased it yourself, we're glad you read it! It's just one of the many helpful, insightful, and encouraging resources produced by Focus on the Family.

In fact, that's what Focus on the Family is all about—providing inspiration, information, and biblically based advice to people in all stages of life.

It began in 1977 with the vision of one man, Dr. James Dobson, a licensed psychologist and author of 16 best-selling books on marriage, parenting, and family. Alarmed by the societal, political, and economic pressures that were threatening the existence of the American family, Dr. Dobson founded Focus on the Family with one employee—an assistant—and a once-a-week radio broadcast, aired on only 36 stations.

Now an international organization, Focus on the Family is dedicated to preserving Judeo-Christian values and strengthening the family through more than 70 different ministries, including eight separate daily radio broadcasts; television public service announcements; 11 publications; and a steady series of award-winning books, films, and videos for people of all ages and interests.

Recognizing the needs of, as well as the sacrifices and important contribution made by, such diverse groups as educators, physicians, attorneys, crisis pregnancy center staff, and single parents, Focus on the Family offers specific outreaches to uphold and minister to these individuals, too. And it's all done for one purpose, and one purpose only: to encourage and strengthen individuals and families through the life-changing message of Jesus Christ.

• • •

For more information about the ministry, or if we can be of help to your family, simply write to Focus on the Family, Colorado Springs, CO 80995 or call 1-800-A-FAMILY (1-800-232-6459). Friends in Canada may write Focus on the Family, P.O. Box 9800, Stn. Terminal, Vancouver, B.C. V6B 4G3 or call 1-800-661-9800. Visit our Web site—www.family.org—to learn more about the ministry or to find out if there is a Focus on the Family office in your country.

We'd love to hear from you!